CROCODILIAN

A NOVEL BY BRIAN GATTO

SEVEREDPRESS

CROCODILIAN

PART ONE:
HABITO ISLAND

CHAPTER ONE

An impeccable sky.

With the shift from night to early morning casting its rays of light along the horizon, it began. The small island of Habito belonged to a chain of islands. It was the peninsula everyone wanted to live at. Most of the fish ended up trapped in the cove which was a side swim from the current that they traveled. Within the inlet were well-placed nets, lines, and even traps for the crustaceans that too would get sucked in as they crept across the ocean floor just outside the bay.

Further inland was a small village that was constructed to surround the fjord. Habito was not a massive island. Most of its inhabitants were located in small huts and shacks that made up most of the coastal water line. There were occasional waves from passing boats but the weather, for the most part, was tranquil. High tide did not occur often. The last time was thirty years ago in 1946.

What attracted many non-island residents was that amazing sky that came over the cliff faces and graced the village with an array of orange. Some of the papers from Hong Kong would say that the island looked like it got hit with the world's safest atomic bomb.

That was one thing the locals, namely Kenji Ho, despised the most. Kenji did not believe in superstition nor luck but he was grateful they had avoided what Japan had suffered. Living closer to the region of Hong Kong meant the testing was not in their own backyard. Still, that did not mean there were not implications from other government testing.

Kenji sat up in his cot and looked out over the bay. It was going to be another splendid day in terms of weather. Very little seemed to go wrong. It was an easy living, away from all the hustle and bustle, pop and rock of the other territories. They were all influenced by modern culture. That was one thing Kenji could do without.

"Morning." A delicate hand wrapped around his shoulder.

"How'd you sleep?" Kenji asked his wife, Dala.

Dala gave him a side glance and smiled. "*We* slept fine. Like always."

Kenji looked down at her stomach and smiled. The light of their lives was due in a month's time. As far as they were concerned, it could be whenever. Dala's pregnancy had been as smooth sailing as a trip around Habito's cove. He then looked at her. She was of Polish and Filipino descent. Not a local, but rather a tourist.

"I've got to get ready. The fish don't catch themselves."

"They kind of do with those nets you've got out there," Dala smirked.

He chuckled. "Whip up some eggs. I'll get the gear ready."

The two parted only to find that being separate was a freezing endurance test. It was the one downside to Habito. The mornings were blistering cold. Especially in February like they were in now. They both put on slips and went about their duties.

Having lived on the island all his life, Kenji was used to the chill. Dala was having a harder time adjusting. Especially ever since she found out she was pregnant. He told her it was all in her head. She did not think so.

As Dala placed the frying pan atop a grill on the fireplace, she felt a kick. "Oohh."

Kenji was outside, placing his hooks along the rope that hung from the starboard side of his fishing dinghy. He took in a deep breath, embracing the warmth only found by the direct sunlight. At peace.

Dala looked out the window at him. Her voice was just above a whisper. "Kenji."

There was another kick, and she grabbed her stomach. Cursing under her breath, she made her way over to the doorway. It was a slow process with each step bringing newfound pain to her abdomen. Eventually, she could not take any more and fell to the ground on her hands. She looked up at Kenji who had already shoved off and was more than fifty yards out.

Dala let out a sharp breath as a single tear fell from her eye. A sudden, newfound determination came over her. She had to do this by herself. There was no one who would come to her aid. The nearest hut was well over a mile away. No matter how much she screamed, she doubted anyone could hear her. Even if by some chance they could, they were probably already out fishing.

Collapsing onto her backside, she began to take in quick sharp breaths. Preforming Lamaze came naturally. She felt it begin to push and she reached for the nearby bed sheet. As she quickly placed it in her mouth, her water broke. There was a brief relief followed by an impossible pain.

"Gah!"

She tried not to open her mouth too wide in order to keep the sheet in place. Sweat spilled down her face as did tears. The chill of the morning provided no relief. Then, she pushed. Each time felt like knives cutting up her insides. Begging inwardly for the sweet release of this nightmare, she pushed again. She could not believe something so small could cause this much agony. Still, she had no choice. This baby was coming whether she liked it or not.

Pushing again, she heard something. It reminded her of when Kenji would fillet fish. The mushy noise continued until a new sound came about. A cry.

She looked down and began to cry with joy. The baby lay there on a blanket that she did not even realize she had lay on. The crying was followed by soft coughs as the infant tried to breathe on its own.

Before she could even grab it, it managed to allow oxygen to flow into its lungs. When she had it in her arms, she realized it was a boy.

She looked up to the ceiling, her mind going past it. Towards the heavens. Smiling, she thanked whoever may be up there.

The sound of water sloshing on stone caught Dala's attention first. It was the same calming cacophony of noise that signified that Kenji was home. He had been out most of the day. As she watched him grab his little wooden cooler box, she became overjoyed. He only brought it out if he had an impressive catch to show her.

He then grabbed a line of fish that ran one after the other on a thin wire. Continuing to gather his supplies, he smiled to himself and shook his head.

"Dala, you won't believe what I found," he called to her.

She walked to the doorway and smiled. "You won't believe what I had."

Kenji did not look at her but rather the box. He shook his head again. "This right here is truly unusual. I just can't figure out how..."

There was a sudden cry. It sounded like a baby. His head snapped upward and he looked at Dala. She looked like she had lost a little weight and was fatigued. He nearly dropped the box as he stumbled over a rock.

"Be careful! You'll wake him," she giggled.

"Him?" He choked back his tears.

He walked slowly up to their hut as Dala held out her hands. He took them carefully as she guided him inside. Over by the fireplace, wrapped in a bundle of blankets, was their son. He let go of Dala and covered his mouth in astonishment.

"When?"

"Right after you left." Dala smiled.

Kenji approached his son slowly and knelt down. He gently scooped him up. The tears were becoming nearly impossible to hold back. "He's beautiful."

Dala came up to him and rested her head on his shoulder. "He's ours."

It was well into the night when Dala became more awake. She had been sleeping with the baby most of the day. Kenji was sitting next to her on the bed. Between them was their son.

"What did we decide for a name?"

"Dawid," she answered.

"I thought it was Hai?"

"Hmm. I don't know. I like both."

She thought about it some more. The infant hiccupped and she gave it a gentle shake. He stopped. She could not believe how small he was. Especially for how much effort it was to push him out. It was no small feat. *The miniature wonder.*

"Hai sounds perfect." She strained her neck to kiss her husband.

Both of them moved closer together to keep themselves and Hai warm.

"What does Hai mean in Chinese?" Dala asked.

"Ocean or sea."

"Oh," she whispered. "Then I feel we've made the right choice in naming him that."

"Me too." Kenji was barely responsive as he was beginning to drift off into sleep.

Dala was feeling the effects of his exhaustion. He gave a mighty yawn which drained her even further. She fought not to repeat the infectious act.

"Ahhh," Hai squeaked.

"Aw." Dala looked from him to Kenji. "Like father, like son."

It was early morning when Dala awoke. Outside was dim with the blue sky beginning to take over with a faint hue. She reached for Hai and felt his chest rising and falling slowly. She then reached for Kenji but he was not there.

The sound of a pot being kicked and spinning across the floor caught her attention and she looked up. Kenji was there but his mind was elsewhere.

"What is it?"

"I'm trying to find that container."

"Which one?"

"The one with the crocodile in it."

"Crocodile?" Her eyebrow arched.

"Yes. I wanted to show it to you yesterday but was obviously busy with something more important." There was no regret in his voice.

Kenji was never one to get testy and she loved that about him. Still, when he set his mind to something, he could get distracted easily.

"Want me to help you find it?"

"No, that's alright. Stay with Hai." He continued to search. "I'm sure I put it here somewhere. I could've sworn it was right by the door."

"Maybe the wind picked it up and brought it outside?" Dala suggested. "How big was the crocodile?"

"Less than six inches." He made his way to the door. "I just don't want it to get out and cause any problems."

Dala knew what he meant. She had heard stories of animals taking small children or feasting upon them as they slept. She could not fathom what she would do if a baby crocodile attacked Hai.

"Hand me the flashlight, please," Kenji asked.

They always kept a flashlight on either side of the mattress in case of emergencies. She grabbed it and handed it to him.

"Thanks." He flicked it on.

Outside turned black again with the intrusion of light coming from the torch. Kenji pointed it at the doorway and then shone it further up. The light cast onto the stone pebbled beach, and he saw it.

"Ah, there it is."

He walked over and picked it up. The small chest was sealed, and he felt the extra weight of the reptile inside. Still, he wanted to make sure it was alive. He carefully unlatched straps and opened the top. The animal lay motionless.

It stared at him with cold, unblinking eyes; in fact, the nictating lenses were covering half of its eyes. He reached down. "I'm sorry, little one."

Petting the top of its head, he said a short prayer before pulling back. He then walked the chest over to the shoreline. Dumping the contents, which not only included the crocodile but a few fish scraps that had been clearly munched on, he waited until it was entirely empty.

"Is everything alright?" Dala called to him.

Kenji did not answer. He stared at the lifeless crocodile bobbing in the water.

Wraaaggh.

A strange chirping noise could be heard. He looked up and noticed a similar sized reptile darting on the surface. It moved back and forth with urgency. He then saw that it was another crocodile.

"I can't watch this," he said softly and marched back up to the hut.

The infantile crocodilian swam up to its sibling, bopped it a couple of times with its tiny snout, and then clamped its jaws around its midsection. Then, both reptiles disappeared below the surface, a slick trail of dark blood in their wake.

CHAPTER TWO

A second life.

News of Kenji and Dala's child had reached the local population of Habito that very next day. Kenji's parents, his father Yang, and mother Tao, were the first to know. None of Dala's relatives lived on the island so, to her, everyone on the island was family.

The Ho family also extended to a younger brother named Zihan and a great grandmother named Daiyu. She was named after the black jade gem because, without her father discovering it, Habito would not have been a village that they knew it as now. She paid for most of everything and was a representative of sorts.

When wind caught of Kenji falling for an outsider, she was hesitant. She still was to an extent. Wise beyond her years, she still could not relinquish the old ways. Then the outsider was with child. His child. She had no choice but to accept the way things were.

Times were changing whether anyone believed it or not. Dala was proof of that.

Next to know was the priest, Father Po. He offered to baptize the child the following morning. It was not until much later in the day that there was word of another birthing. Krang and his wife, Caiji, were not expecting for another week. Time meant nothing to the child. It was decided then that there would be two baptisms.

Both proud parents of healthy boys.

Krang and Kenji decided to go fishing together early the next morning. They knew of each other beforehand but not personally.

"I feel it's a sign," Krang told Kenji sincerely.

"A sign?" The look of disbelief in Kenji's eyes was electrifying. "You believe in signs?"

"I believe in a lot of things. I believe there are forces at work that propel good and evil. In this case," Krang leaned forward on the rickety dinghy, "I feel our boys were born so close together for a reason."

"What are you driving at?"

"I am just saying. It would be a dishonor to ignore such telltale signs."

"What signs? You keep speaking in riddles."

"One day, Kenji, maybe you will understand." Krang said, patting him on the back

On shore, in the shack, Dala and Caiji were changing the boys' diapers. Tao was watching from the corner of the room. She liked Dala well enough but she was very much inexperienced in the field of motherhood.

She remembered when Kenji was born. She herself caught on pretty quickly. She hoped Dala would do the same.

Dala turned and looked at how Caiji was preparing the pin on the diaper. It seemed so complex just to keep it in place.

"Have you had children before?" Dala asked her.

"No. Well, that's not entirely true. I had a miscarriage a few years ago."

"Oh. I'm sorry."

"It's no worry. Our son will fill that void."

'I suppose so." Dala smiled.

"It's the truth!" Caiji was rather spontaneous with her response. She seemed like she said it by accident but did not care.

"I believe you," Dala said.

"Don't believe in me. Believe in your child."

"Trust me. We have high hopes for him." Dala lifted Hai up and his diaper slipped off his legs.

"Here, let me help you." Tao approached.

She then went over the process and Dala watched her intensely. She knew that Kenji's mother was strict, so she wanted to get it right the first time after she was told.

Caiji finished. She then stood up and walked away from the table. Tao had just finished pinning the diaper.

"Make sense?" she asked.

Dala nodded and Tao undid it again.

"Show me," she said as she allowed her daughter-in-law to fix up the diaper.

As soon as she started, Tao smiled. "You catch on quick for a tourist."

"Kenji told you about that?" she inquired.

"Everyone here knows, sweetie." Tao smiled and brushed her cheek.

"You're the first outsider to take up permanent residence in Habito."

"Is that so?" Dala said, intrigued.

"You have a lot to learn about small communities. Didn't you come from the United States?"

"Yes. Boston, actually. I was on a college field trip and decided to never go back."

"You only know city life?" Caiji asked as she poured a cup of tea from the kettle on the grill over the firepit.

"I've been here for long enough. Although, I didn't know crocodiles were indigenous to the area."

Caiji nearly dropped her tea.

"What did you just say?" Tao looked horrified. It was as if a ghost from the past had suddenly walked through the front door and right by Dala.

"Kenji. He found a baby crocodile two days ago on his morning fishing trip."

"That's not possible." Tao maintained her cold, dead stare.

"It's okay. When he went to show it to me, it was dead."

Caiji almost dropped her baby next.

"Careful!" Dala cried.

"I don't want it! Get it away from me!" Caiji handed Dala the baby and ran out of the hut.

"Caiji! Caiji, come back!" Dala cried out. "Tao, do something!"

Her mother-in-law sat there, mumbling a prayer.

Dala tried to run after Caiji but, by the time she got outside, she saw she was already in Krang's arms crying.

Kenji looked equally as confused. "What's going on? What happened?"

"I told her about the crocodile you found."

"Oh geeze," Kenji sighed. "Caiji. It was just a baby."

"It's a sign!" Krang shouted.

"Enough of you and your signs!" Kenji nearly screamed at him. "You're scaring everyone."

"What does it mean? To find a baby crocodile?"

Tao suddenly appeared in the doorway. "If one is to find a crocodilian and let it die, a curse will be cast for all of time."

"It didn't die alone!" Kenji stated.

"Dala said you didn't have a chance to show it to her. How could it not have died alone?"

"It may not have died. I let it go and another one came by and took it."

"Did it nurture it, or eat it?"

"I don't know. I didn't stick around. It's all nonsense anyway. Just silly superstition."

Tao shook her head slowly. "My poor boy. You may have just doomed us all. The worst part is you don't believe it."

Krang and Caiji both walked over to Dala.

"Keep him safe," Caiji told her.

"It's not my child." Dala was not ready to handle a second baby. She could barely change the diapers of one.

"Take him, Caiji," Krang said. "We must leave the village in the night."

Caiji reached for her child and took him. "I pray you all do the same."

The young couple then made their way up the slope and towards the other huts.

***

The night was filled with animosity. Tao had left shortly after Krang and Caiji did. For most of the rest of the day, Kenji and Dala remained apart. They did not ignore each other, continuously staring with longing eyes. Something kept them apart though. Some sort of external force.

Neither of them sensed it. Kenji did not believe in such spiritual emotions while Dala did not know of the traditions, customs, or beliefs. She was the outsider: an aloof trespasser to the ways of the village.

Despite everyone welcoming her, she felt isolated. At first there were times she would cry herself to sleep. Kenji's father put an end to that by rallying up everyone and commencing with a prayer for acceptance.

It was a beautiful moment that felt warranted. Even if Kenji and Yang were the only two who really seemed interested in their performance.

Night fell and, again, Dala cried. She had not sobbed so deeply in a long time. Kenji came over to her as she looked for guidance in understanding. He knew there was no way to help her understand unless taught.

He coddled her by embracing her in a tight grip and showering her with kisses atop her head. Her black hair was a bit matted with sweat and the heat had not helped. To him though, she still looked as beautiful as ever.

"Do you remember when we first met?"

Dala nodded. "I saw you through my camera lens."

"And I saw this stranger taking a picture of me just as I was pulling my cages." He smiled. "Do you remember what the first thing you said to me was?"

She sniffled. "I was an idiot and spoke English."

"I thought it was Polish or Filipino?"

"Good thing I knew Chinese,." she giggled.

"You're smart, Dala. Being the smartest one in your class doesn't make you an expert on everything."

"I would hope to not be an expert on everything." She took a deep breath. "Ever since I came here, I felt at peace with myself. For the first time, now, I'm beginning to have doubts."

"Doubts?"

"Maybe we should leave Habito."

"Then my parents would think something is up. Plus, I can't leave. I want to see my brother Zihan grow up."

"What about Hai. I don't want to take him away from a place he becomes familiar with."

"This is a discussion I feel you've wanted to talk about for a long time."

She turned her cheek. "I can't say that that's not true."

"Oh, Dala," Kenji sighed. "Zihan turns sixteen tomorrow. After that, we will pack up and leave."

"No. We don't have to. I don't want to ruin your livelihood."

"I am sure there are plenty of jobs in Boston."

She placed a gentle hand on his face. "I love you."

"I love you. I can't believe how beautiful you are."

Dala traced her hand down Kenji's bare chest until eventually finding her way inside his trousers. She stroked his shaft slowly and then began to pull his undergarment down.

"Whaaaa!"

The two looked away from each other. Hai was sobbing now.

"I best go see what he wants."

"I'll be here." Kenji held her hand as she got up.

"Hopefully not for too much longer." She gave him an awkward smile. "That didn't come out right."

"It's alright. I knew what you meant." Kenji gave a head tilt, telling her to tend to their son.

She strode over and checked on him. He was fast asleep. "Bad dreams."

***

Not far from the village, Father Po sat in his church. It stood near the edge of the peninsula. He was looking over scriptures and preparing for the double ceremony tomorrow when he heard the door creak open.

"Hello?"

"It's me, Father. Krang."

"Well, Krang. It is quite late, and services are not until the morning. I know you and Caiji are excited, but I must insist you go home and get some rest."

"I need to talk to someone, and I don't think anyone else will understand."

"What troubles you, my child?"

"The signs. Everything is pointing to catastrophe."

"What signs?"

"The crocodile that showed up."

"What crocodile?"

Krang relayed what had transpired two mornings ago. Father Po nodded. "I see."

"With such an occurrence, how could one chalk it up to coincidence?"

Father Po did not say a word as he got up and made his way into his chambers. It was a small room, but books covered most of the wall space. He pulled one down. "I remember you borrowing this one a lot as a child. You must have read it a dozen times. I doubt, however, that you read the copyright."

As the priest opened the book, Krang approached and then peered over his shoulder.

"1932 is the copyright for this book, which, if you read further, the story of The Great Crocodile was first conceived in 1742 by an old sea witch."

"Who was she?"

"I have no idea. You read the book," Father Po chuckled.

"Why would she make up such a fantastic story?"

"First of all, Krang, sea witches are not of the sea. They are witches that live by the sea. Secondly, witchcraft such as theirs has been ruled out even by other witches. There is no reason to believe Armageddon will happen."

He closed the book and went to put it back on the shelf.

"I've been hearing voices," Krang said suddenly.

Freezing in place, Father Po did not know what to say at first. All he could think to do was repeat the man. "Voices?"

"They've been telling me to watch out for signs."

"I don't think I fully understand, my child."

Krang began to back out of the room. "You will, Father. You all will."

When the priest heard the door to his church finally shut, he ran to his liquor cabinet and pulled out some unlabeled beverage. He had been saving it for a special occasion. It was one he discovered at a trade show. One sip was all it took for him to trade other booze and some fish for it.

He did not bother grabbing a glass. He popped the cork off the bottle and gave it a steady chug. When he relinquished his lips from the savory liquid, he looked down at himself. "This cannot be."

Marching back into his chambers, he shut the squeaky door as quietly as he could.

Pulling the book from the shelf once more, he opened it. He found the pages dedicated to the great crocodile and devoured its contents. When he finished, he slammed the book closed and mumbled prayers he had not spoken since he was a boy.

CHAPTER THREE

Rising with the sun.

Kenji Ho sat up from the mattress in a downpour of sweat. The salt stung his eyes. Droplets fell down his face and from his chin. He could not believe what he had dreamt. The idea seemed too preposterous. There was no way such a force of nature would wipe out Habito.

Dala turned on her side and noticed the position he was in and how tense his body was. She carefully placed a hand on his arm, trying not to startle him. It had the opposite effect. His head snapped in her direction.

"We must leave!" he told her.

"What?"

He quickly got off the bed and began to search around the room for their personal artifacts, collecting them as he went.

"What are you doing?" Dala asked worriedly.

"I just had a vision."

"You had a nightmare."

"Nightmares aren't that real," he responded feverishly.

"Just come back to bed and tell me what happened in this *vision*."

He shut one of the drawers on their dresser and stood there looking at his reflection in the small mirror. "There's no time."

"There's always time," she replied.

Kenji stepped back and nearly fell onto the mattress. He was able to stop himself, falling forward onto his knees. "It was like Armageddon."

"The end of times?" Dala asked.

"It was a sea of horror," Kenji began. "The ocean swelled with violent currents that tore through Habito. Standing atop the cove rock wall was a man I have never met. He held, in his hand, our baby. The water soon rose up to him and Hai and he sacrificed himself to save Hai. The debris tore through him like tissue paper. Hai was left all alone as the water descended."

Dala got off the mattress and inched closer to him. "Just dreams."

He looked to her. "Or a prophetic vision."

***

A clustered ceremony was about to begin. The small church was filled with local villagers as they gathered around to experience the paedobaptism. The christening event was to start at any moment. A joyous celebration, if only Father Po was near.

No one found the missing priest to be as much a conundrum as Kenji. He was always at the doors to let people in during these kinds of events. Krang and Yang had to push the doors apart with brute force. Once inside, the place had not been decorated or prepared at all.

It looked the same as it had the night before, Krang thought. *Maybe the old fool really did heed his warning and abandoned them.*

"Where is he, Dad?" Kenji turned to Yang.

"I'm not sure. Father Po is never one to miss a ceremony. Let alone two in one day."

There came a sudden, shrill scream.

"Caiji!" Krang shouted and ran outside to investigate.

Kenji followed. They sprinted side by side yet both had very different feelings as to what they would find. Kenji expected to see Father Po dead from alcohol poisoning. Krang wondered if Caiji was screaming at Father Po for assaulting her. He never liked the way the elder priest looked at his wife.

They were both half right.

Father Po was attacking Caiji, though not in a drunken state. His face and fingers were badly mutilated.

"Hey!" Kenji ran down to him first, trying to beat Krang from hurting him more so than he already was.

Caiji was covered in Father Po's blood and some strands of sinew. She fell back and rolled around on the ground, gripping her baby close to her chest.

"The baby. It must perish!" Father Po muttered through his gore-caked lips.

"Get away from her, you fool!" Krang shouted.

Kenji pulled the priest back.

Father Po just stared at them with whatever he had for eyes left. He then reached down into his robe and revealed a small animal, a crocodile. "We're all doomed."

He then raised the reptile to his neck and let it snap down on his throat. It made quick work of his jugular as it tore it out, letting blood release in a gushing flow.

Caiji screamed as she looked upon the priest. His life fluids sprayed out in a blanket of blood that coated her in a juicy splatter.

"Get her out of here," Kenji demanded.

Krang did not hesitate. As he dragged her away, he kept whispering, "I only meant to scare him."

***

The sea seemed to have a new meaning to Krang. He had been invited to go out with a fellow fisherman named Ching to try and bag some extra catch. Yet he declined the offer and, rather than stay in the village with Caiji and their newborn, he rowed out towards the border rock wall of the inlet.

There was an insidious atmosphere that crept in with the current, the undertow pushed all the horrors into the area. It was as if the sea was flushing all the problems in the outside world in. Krang did not feel welcome anymore. Tears streamed down his face as he stared up at the gargantuan cliff face.

He quickly gathered some supplies. It was fishing gear and a bundle of cloth. The contents were barely recognizable to him anymore. He then found a solid foundation and placed his foot on the slippery surface. His sandals had ridges underneath, so they helped him maintain a grip on the rocks.

With the supplies slung over his back, and his mind set, he began to climb. There was the feeling that something was calling to him, like a ghostly apparition wailing to summon him to the top.

It had only been an hour since the priest killed himself. It was going to be another hour when another horrific act would be performed.

Seldomly did he look down at the waves brushing up against the rocks. He could hear them in the back of his mind but did not fully register them. As he ascended higher, the noises of the sea were becoming less apparent. Further up, he felt the wind blow through his unkempt black hair.

He felt as though he was leaving the sea behind to rise to another level of consciousness. Many would call it witchcraft or possession, he found it cathartic. It purified his senses and drove him higher.

Further and further did he climb. There was no understanding of how far he had come or how much further he had to go. To Krang, it was all sacrificial to understand the higher power that beckoned him.

With bated breath, he continued onward. The fulfilment would be gratifying to him. He smiled as he went, a devilish smile creeping across his thin lips. He began to laugh at each stone that slipped out from under him, or wet spot that tried to make him descend back to the sea below. That cursed entrapment that contained no oxygen.

It was a prison for him. He had to escape. There was no stalling. No break needed. He was going to reach the epiphany and go beyond.

Soon there was no more rock to climb. He hurled himself atop a smooth surface among the jagged rocks and set himself down to accept a generous amount of fresh, salty air.

He was ready.

Caiji awoke with a start. She felt something was off, missing in her life. After blinking a couple of times, trying to clear her vision, she became acutely aware that something was wrong. Krang was not in their hut.

She felt down by her side and then froze in abstract fear. Their baby was missing too. Her already pale skin took on a new shade of milky white. She began to hyperventilate.

"This has gone too far." Caiji stood up suddenly.

Krang did not believe in such silly superstitions. Did he? She began to wonder how much she actually knew about her husband. It was in that moment that the first shouts and hollers could be heard outside.

Practically leaping off the bed, she made her way over towards the doorway. She saw a few of the fishermen and their wives pointing up near the left cliff that bordered the cove. There, standing tall and proud, was Krang.

"No!" Caiji's face morphed into one of abstract terror.

Before anyone could get to their boats to paddle out and attempt to stop him, whatever he was doing, Krang held out a bundle of cloth.

Caiji nearly fainted.

Kenji and Dala were only starting to pack the essentials. They would leave the village by midday and never look back. Hai watched them scurry around the hut. His attention was held only briefly by their rampant rummaging. Soon, he drifted into a light sleep.

It was when Kenji picked up an old photo of his grandparents, true villagers in every sense of the word, that they heard the screaming. Dala dropped the frying pan which awakened Hai with a startle.

The alarmed look on Hai's face was accompanied by a tense cry. His eyes were tightly closed as he bellowed out in fright. His mother ran to him to comfort him. She scooped him up in her arms and rocked him back and forth while singing a lullaby.

"What was that?" Dala inquired.

"It sounded like Caiji," Kenji said as he made his way over towards the doorway.

He noticed his father was running up to their hut. Yang had never looked so terrified.

"What is happening?" Kenji ran out to meet him.

"It's Krang," his father said between deep breaths. "He's standing atop the rocks. We think he has his son with him!"

"What! Why?" Kenji asked but Yang turned and ran back to Tao who was trying to catch up.

"Stay here, Dala!" Kenji shouted as he ran after his parents.

Dala did not object. She was as visibly tense as the child she cradled in her arms.

By the time they made it to the launch area, the canoes were already all gone. Several of the fishermen were heading out to stop the possible event that would occur. The legend was becoming more and more true with every passing moment.

Kenji's grandmother, Daiyu, sat by the water's edge. She was mumbling a prayer feverishly, clutching a small artifact tightly in her grasp.

"Hurry up!" Zihan shouted at the top of his lungs. It was no way to start his birthday. As far as he was concerned, a death was a bad omen, not only for himself, but for the village. He was more fearful for the baby than anything else.

He heard his brother and parents approaching and spun on his heels. "It looks like they might make it before he does something crazy!"

The fishermen were indeed very close to the edge of the cove. The rocks were no more than twenty feet away from the nearest boat. Daiyu clutched the artifact tightly and stopped praying. She had done all she could.

Krang looked down at his son. Something within him lacked empathy while his human side tried to push through. It allowed for a single tear to fall from his face before he let go of his son with one hand. With it now free, he reached into his loose-fitting pants and withdrew a hook.

Do it, a voice told him. It sounded like an old evil hag of the sea. *Do it! Do it now before they stop you!*

He could not hear the voices shouting at him from below. The wind was a terrible force. Up there was only him, his child, his hook, and the voices in his head.

Do it before it comes to do it for you!

"We're all dead," Krang told the voice.

I will make it spare you.

"Zihan, grab Father's gun!" Kenji ordered his little brother.

At first, he did not budge. He ordered him again, shouting this time. Zihan did as he was told.

"Hurry!" Yang ordered.

There was no time to lose. The storm would come and so too would the beast. Krang knew it was only a matter of time. They would all die, and he would live. He knew it was selfish but there was no other way. He had to carry it on. Habito had to live on through him.

He placed the tip of the hook on the baby's head and began to slowly press.

The fishermen below were halfway up the rocks.

"No!" one of them shouted.

Krang stopped pressing down and looked over the ledge. There were five of them. They all climbed like crabs scurrying across a beach. Moving fast, they would reach him in no time.

Do it!

"Don't do it, Krang!"

He blinked a couple of times as he felt the rush of guilt flushing through him. He felt limp, like his legs were giving out. They wobbled as he trembled where he stood.

"He's going to drop the boy!"

Indeed, Krang had already loosened his grip enough to lose the hook. It went spiraling down the rocks, nearly hitting one of the fishermen on the head on the way down.

Then it happened.

A shot rang through the air as it struck Krang in the neck. His head snapped one way as his body began to slump over. The baby immediately felt as if he weighed tons. He was too much to carry and his father let him go.

Krang fell backwards as he plummeted into the sea below.

All of the fishermen reached out to try and catch the infant. Some even fell off the cliff face as a result. None were successful.

Caiji stood in stunned silence as she watched both her husband tip back and disappear off one side of the cliff and their newborn child down the other. Her eyes seemed to flicker a bit, as if she was losing her battle with lucidity. Yang and Tao ran up behind her as she slumped down.

Kenji lowered the rifle to his side. He too was feeling the effects of what just happened. His legs trembled and he collapsed onto his hands and knees, the rifle discarded.

Zihan was rigid with disbelief. He had never seen anything as morbid in his sixteen years of life. It was such a cruel act. *Who or what could allow such a thing?* he wondered as he raised his hands towards his face and began to weep.

Daiyu was the only one who seemed to have any strength left. She stood up and marched back towards her hut. It was the furthest one from the water and decorated with all sorts of trinkets. She walked by a couple of strung up gemstones and pushed them out of her face.

Dala had run back inside when Kenji took the shot. There was nothing more to see. It was horrible. She did not want to see the outcome, and, in that, she felt weak. It was almost as if she could not bear the thought of seeing a familiar face or friend leaving this world. It was the same as when she had her dog put down. She had to leave the room just as the drugs kicked in to put her to sleep. She could only imagine what went through the animal's mind. *Why do I feel funny? Why is everything going dark? Why is my owner leaving me?* She placed Hai on their bed and wept for hours.

CHAPTER FOUR

Nature's balance.

A sign that things were changing came from the skies that night. They had become furious with clouds that seemed to fight gravity and attempted to plummet to the earth only to fall back. The sky was black with hints of red. An angry red that was not pleasing to the eye. It was similar to fire and brimstone. The clouds from hell.

Zihan had awoken from a deep sleep. A familiar sound had begun to pelt atop their hut. It was not faint. Rather it was a wall of noise. At first it was just deafening. Then it became aggressive. He tried to close it out by covering his ears but it only seemed to intensify as if he created a funnel for the noise to travel through.

In the next room over, Tao and Yang were suffering a similar experience. It was louder than any rain they had ever encountered before. Yang tried to cover his wife to try and shield her from the droplets seeping through the thatched roof. She was already off the bed though and marching out of the room.

Tao ran across the kitchen area and towards the doorway. When she looked outside, she saw the ocean. It was not as it once had been for so many years. The tranquil waters were now alive with roaring waves that soared high and crashed with explosive results of water spray.

Zihan ran up behind his mother. "What is happening?"

"I... I don't know," she practically whispered.

The sea rose higher and higher, then drew back. It was as if something was pulling the water away from them.

"It's coming!" Daiyu shouted from her hut.

"What is?" One of the villagers exited his own home to run up to the old sage.

She did not respond. Instead, she clutched her gems in her hand and prayed.

"What is happening, damn you?" the villager responded in rage.

"It's Armageddon." Caiji came up towards them. "Just like Krang feared."

"That's nonsense! It's just bad weather," he screamed at her to cover the sound of something roaring.

The waves had been loud but this sound was even more brash and distinct. It was similar to that of a train horn, but it had a guttural touch to it. As if it were alive.

"Heaven Almighty," the villager said to himself and then ran back inside to get his wife and children ready to leave.

"There is no escape. It's coming!" Daiyu cackled like some kind of witch.

Caiji paid no mind as she slowly made her way back to her hut. She had no one to save and decided to accept her and Habito's fate and wait it out.

Dala was the first to waken when the thunder came. Lightning had flashed with menace across the sky. It promised a show to follow. Then came the crack of thunder. It was immense and powerful. She quickly gathered her baby just as Kenji woke with a startle.

He quickly ran to the door and saw that most of the villagers were outside.

"What's happening?" he screamed.

They were too far to hear.

His brother and parents were closest to them. He tried to call for them, but they could not hear him. They were standing by the doorway looking out towards the sea.

"What is happening? What is going-"

There was no finishing the sentence. He had noticed just then that the water had receded tremendously. Now it was coming back.

Everyone stood in silent shock as the wave came at them full force. It rushed over them like a baptism by drowning. The wall of water was so immense that it had nearly towered over the rocks near the inlet and now it was over the village of Habito.

As fast as it had covered the village, it returned out. It took with it people, huts, and other debris. The cataclysmic event was not complete. The water returned for a second dousing.

Zihan had grabbed onto his parents and pushed them back inside. When the rush of the dirty sea came it did not matter. It took them and the entire hut out to sea.

Kenji could only watch as his family home and others like it were swept out with the current. He could not speak. He could only look on in despair.

The skies above looked like angry balls of cotton, black and misshapen. They moved in an unnatural way. As if hell had conquered heaven and was pushing its way back down to earth.

Daiyu noticed this and decided to accept her fate. There was no hope. It was all for naught. Prayer would only be laughed at by the demonic energy that had slammed into Habito.

Then came the roar again.

Caiji did not care what was to come when it came to the weather. What came out of the sea though, that caught her attention as it did for everyone else who saw it.

The scaly menace crawled onto the beach. It dragged its massive frame uphill until it was level with what remained of the village. Its red eyes narrowed onto the hapless people.

Kenji could only stare in disbelief. It was a crocodile, only bigger than it had any right to be. He gaged from the tip of its ridged snout to the end of its barnacle-laden tail that it was around thirty meters in length.

"This cannot be," he said in disbelief.

"Oh, god," Dala said softly.

Behind the crocodile, a whirl of wind began to swirl up. It seemed to come from nowhere, generated by an invisible force. The reptile let out a low, guttural roar and the wind came down on the village.

It hit what remained of their neighbors' huts first. Caiji was picked up off the ground and flung for miles. Daiyu closed her eyes even though she knew it was hopeless. It came at her at full force and sent her flying back into her hut. It then dismantled the structure piece by piece until it was all taken in the wind.

The raging rampage continued as Kenji turned and grabbed Dala who was holding Hai tightly.

Then, they were hit too. It felt like shards of glass slicing into Kenji's back. The pain was unbearable, and he tried to fight through it. Eventually, he had to let go and, when he did, he fell to the ground. He peered up with blurry vision as he saw Dala's hair whipping in the wind, her baggy clothing becoming tattered. She was then lifted off the ground and carried into the storm.

"Ahhhh!" Kenji cried in absolute horror. "No! No! No! Dala! Hai!"

They were gone. As soon as he could not see them anymore, the storm died. The last thing he heard before slipping into unconsciousness was the sound of the crocodile roaring and then sloshing sounds as it made its way back into the sea.

***

Morning had arrived and it was as peaceful as any other morning on Habito. If not for the catastrophic damage to the village, it would have been another normal day. The sky was blue, and the clouds were spaced out and as white as a sheet.

Kenji awoke with a start. He felt woozy but did not care. He looked for a solid foundation to lift himself off the ground with. He grabbed onto the table that was as level as the bed but more supportive than the mattress. It was as if the storm stopped right over their hut and died.

Some of his home had not been touched. The most important pieces were missing though.

"Dala, Hai?" He choked as he spoke their names.

He hoped they would come out of the rubble, not a scratch on them. Instead, there was silence up to the sea where the noisy waves brushed against the beach.

Kenji turned to look. What he saw made his blood run cold. It could not be. It had been there and was very real. His life had not been an illusion.

Besides a few planks that could be considered driftwood, the village was completely gone. There was not a trace of the structures or the people who had lived in them. It was as if they had been wiped off the map, erased from history.

Kenji made his way over to where his parents and brother's shack was. There were no remnants. The only thing he found was at his grandmother's house. It was the gems she had strung up. They were attached to a piece of wood that had once been her doorway. He held them close.

After a brief search, he made his way back to his home. There was nothing beyond it. Just a white, sandy beach and some dunes which were the next place he looked.

He went up and down the slopes for a few hundred feet. There was nothing to gain from it. They had all disappeared without a trace. There was no hope.

The wounds on his back stung so he decided to head back to the hut. He tried to pat them down with a cloth, but they were mostly scabs and would only bleed the more he rubbed them. He sat back and placed his hands on his face. Tears streaked down it as he contemplated what to do next.

In that moment, he heard something. It was a gurgled cry. Kenji stood up immediately and ran outside. The sound was coming from close to the shore. He did not see anyone right away. It was not until his eyes fell upon a piece of driftwood that he noticed a bundle sitting there.

He sprinted towards it. "Hai!"

Scooping up the bundle in his arms, he was practically smothering the child. He then pulled back and began to peel away the cloth.

It was not Hai. It was Caiji and Krang's child.

He did not know what to think or say. All he could do was walk back to his hut and find something to nourish him with.

After a few minutes, he found nothing. He then gathered up some supplies and marched out into the dunes. He knew there was a radio tower not too far away. They were not completely cut off but preferred to live as if so.

He began his journey, hopeful. There was not only proof that he was not alone and that there was a village there, but that the curse was not real. The child had in fact not been successfully sacrificed.

The trek was hard. He knew he had garnered a few blisters along the way. The morning haze had worn off and it was nearing afternoon. It was by this time that he started to see the outline of the radio tower. It was still standing. He said a prayer of thanks and picked up the pace.

Eventually, he managed to reach it and put out a call for a pickup.

They arrived a couple of hours later by chopper. There was a search for others. The next day they had brought in a dredger and found body parts and pieces of the huts in the channel. Some still clung to the rocks as if they did not want to leave their lives behind.

A week later and Kenji found himself standing outside an orphanage. He looked down at the child in his arms. Caiji and Krang had not named him. He found it in poor taste to wait. Still, he could not accept the responsibility. After losing Dala and Hai, he almost wanted to give up on life. What could he provide for this child? How could he cope with everything and raise someone else's kid?

It was settled. He placed the child in a basket with a note and rang the doorbell. He then walked away and did not look back.

PART TWO:
ONE YEAR LATER

CHAPTER ONE

The chariot of steel.

Morgan Stanley was 36,000 feet in the air and loving every minute of it. He was a doctor by trade and a damn proud one at that. There were no bad reviews flowing in nor publicity that would be damaging to his career. He had been trustworthy, never one to take people's money for minor appointments.

His colleagues did not understand his methods, but he was making a killing. This rang especially true for the honesty policy he had in place at his office back in America. He would let people pay him when they had secured the funds to afford their operations. There was no rush. No immediate demand for dollars.

Last week he had received a letter from an old friend. Yow Wang Chung was a fellow doctor, with a PHD in biology. The human anatomy was his playground. He was not a mad scientist, just a curious one. They had gone to the same school and struck up a friendship over time. His English was very commendable having his roots be in Hong Kong.

Morgan thought back on what Yow had told him about his language barrier or lack thereof. He was a firm believer in the art of communication and, if he could not talk to people, then what was the point in being a doctor. Yow had studied several languages besides English, including French, German, Italian, and Japanese. He knew he had many more to go but had become fascinated with tribal languages like those found in Africa.

The plane gave a slight shudder, and everyone jumped. Morgan was relaxed. He had been on dozens of plane rides this year alone. He planned to be on at least ten more to greet the year 1978 with a new record to beat.

Slowly, the aircraft righted itself and the pilot spoke Chinese into the intercom to relax the passengers. He then switched to English without much trouble. Morgan chuckled, thinking it would be funny if Yow was the pilot. He would not put it past him to become one. The Chung family was very gifted and wanted to cover all bases.

He recalled the last time he met up with Yow. It was when he and his family were in Bangkok to help the lesser folk with medical assistance. It was the first time he had met his family. There was Sang Chung, a beautiful dame of Chinese and African descent. A rare combination but a welcome one. Their daughter, Dede, was a precious infant at that time. It had been well over six years since he had seen her. *She must have grown like a weed,* Morgan thought back with a smile.

There was another woman with them. She was in the background somewhat. An aunt of Yow's he had thought. She was drop dead gorgeous regardless of her age. She was gifted in all the right places. She had firm, rosy cheeks and piercing brown eyes. It all came together with a wide, inviting smile. Morgan snapped out of it as the pilot came on again to tell them they were landing soon.

The ground below began to come into view. It was the morning, and the region was alive with the hustle and bustle of the early crowd. As the plane soared over the airport, Morgan could see how tight traffic was. Everyone was literally bumper to bumper. He hoped Yow was already there. He did not like the feeling of being alone and out of his element.

Once they landed and he entered the airport, he sighed with relief. Over by the windows stood an eager Yow and Sang. Sang pointed to him and the two waved. Morgan excitedly waved back.

Throngs of people drove him towards the food court which is where he met up with them in person.

"Morgan, xiansheng!"

"Oh, cut it with that formal crap!" Morgan held Yow in a tight embrace.

Once they parted, he repeated the gesture with Sang. When they broke apart, Morgan looked to both of them. "How've you two been? It feels like it has been ages!"

"We've been well. Dede is at home with her grandma. She can't wait to see you again."

"Really? I haven't seen her since she was a toddler."

"You must have made an impression. She remembers you," Sang laughed.

"That's swell!" Morgan beamed.

Sang looked to Morgan's side. He only had one suitcase. "Is this all you've brought?"

"Yes. I didn't want to pack too much. Wasn't quite sure how long I was staying."

"Well. You're welcome to stay as long as you want," Sang grinned.

"Come! I've got a cab waiting. If we hurry, we can beat the lunch rush." Yow smiled and the three made their way out of the airport.

***

Splashing was the thing their mother hated the most. She would always tell the three siblings to grow up and not play games while in the pool or open water. They were in their twenties. What did it matter if they had a bit of fun out in the ocean off Kowloon Bay. It was not annoying anyone.

At one point their mother had brought up it was unattractive to other women. That could not be further from the truth. There was one with them right now! The most popular girl at college. The real kicker was that she splashed more than the rest of them.

The youngest of the group, a mere twenty-two years old, began to venture further out. He was not normally so bold, but he felt like playing it cool more than safe today. He laughed as he watched his brothers and the woman rough house. It was not a bad thing, he thought. If their mother were here, she would make it so. He laughed as he lay on his back and floated.

Just as he did so, he felt it. It was like he was rubbing against a rock. He had not felt a reef or any other kind of formation nearby. Nor did he bump into anything. As far as he was concerned, the area was particularly empty save for the fish and other marine life.

A sudden wave, larger than the ones that came before, caused him to rise and fall. He looked down his chest to see the others were still there, preparing themselves for the incoming water. Then he lay back down. He pictured the sea performing some kind of massage on his back. He almost wanted to laugh but realized it was not all that funny. Then it happened again and again. Too fast was the succession of waves. It was unnatural. There had to be a rock formation nearby.

He turned in time to see another wave coming. There was something in it. A pair of jaws so large his mind could not process exactly what it was or how big. They clamped down over his midsection as his legs kicked out.

By the time the others heard the attack, both man and animal were gone. They called for him, inching further out as they did. There was no clear indicator of what had happened. It was not until another wave soared high above them did they see the body, mangled and ravaged, riding the surf. Everyone screamed as it and gallons of water and blood and oodles of innards splashed down atop them.

***

The drive through the city became a test of endurance for Yow and Sang. While they were used to the traffic that covered the streets of Hong Kong on a daily basis, their excitement for seeing Dede's reaction was making them impatient. Not to mention the cab driver's insistence on snapping his gum.

Morgan on the other hand was taking in the sights. There were signs all around that had Chinese written all over as well as English. "There must be a lot of American tourists coming through here."

"Times are changing, my friend," Yow stated. "Even when I was a boy in Thailand, it was becoming prevalent."

"Yes, same with America," Sang added. "It seems like every place is mixing nationalities."

"I guess it was only a matter of time," Morgan said.

Snap.

The cab driver's gum made the sound. It was the loudest one yet.

Yow was getting fed up with it but held his tongue. Morgan noticed his frustration and wanted to mention something to the driver but forced himself to mind his own business. He was not sure how he would react if he told him to stop. Would it be similar to New Yorkers or would there be a level of respect?

Soon they were nearing the beach front properties. Morgan caught glimpses of the sea between houses. It was a crowded area but spaced out enough to not make it feel congested. Some of the houses were practically two-story condos. When the cab pulled into the Chung estate, Morgan was taken aback by the three level home that stood taller than any building in the area.

"This your place?"

"The best money can buy," Yow beamed.

"It's beautiful!"

"With a woman's touch it is. I would not let Yow stay alone for a month. The place would lose its charm, no doubt in my mind," Sang half-heartedly laughed.

When the cab came to a stop, the driver made a big bubble with his gum and let it pop. He then worked it back into his mouth and chewed on any of the leftover air pockets.

Snap. Snap. Snap.

They were not as loud as the previous ones but were aggravating to Yow nevertheless.

"Here we are," the cab driver smiled at them.

The three got out and Yow produced a bundle of Yuan for the driver who grinned and thanked him. With such a minimal amount of luggage, he did not even have to get out to give them a hand. It was an easy and rewarding gig as far as he was concerned.

As he drove away, Yow sighed with relief. "I was ready to pull the gum out of his mouth and toss it out the window."

Morgan chuckled. "It could have been worse. He could have been smoking."

"They do that in New York?" Sang was surprised.

"Sometimes. Not often. Usually, they're parked and waiting for their customers. When they get in the cab smells like a Marlboro factory."

"Wonderful." Yow laughed as he reached into his pockets and produced the keys.

Before they could even ascend the steps, the door swung open. Dede stood there, static. "Uncle Morgan!"

She ran up to him and gave him a hug.

"Well hello to you too!" He returned the embrace.

A woman appeared in the doorway. "I'm sorry. She slipped away from me."

Morgan tried not to look at her and focus on Dede but the woman was just as amazingly beautiful as he remembered. Her shoulder length, wavy black hair shined in the light of the sun, her rosy cheeks blushed with embarrassment yet brought out her features even further. Her smile was warm and cheerful as her eyes squinted a bit from her grin pushing them up.

"I don't know if you remember, this is my mom, Lilly Chung," Yow stated.

"I remember you being there at Dede's birthday party," Morgan told her.

"Good memory. I wasn't there for long. I had to go to court that day. There was no way around it. Divorces, they sure are an ugly thing." She seemed to be looking him over.

"Yes, well." Yow clapped his hands together. "Let's get inside where it's a bit cooler. There was no AC in that cab."

Sang nodded. "It was getting hot in there for sure."

She had noticed how Morgan and Lilly looked at each other almost instantly. She knew there was a spark there, but she was not sure how much Yow would approve.

As they walked inside, Morgan took immediate notice of the décor and furnishings. The walls were yellow with tiny dark brown diamonds covering them. All around the house were trinkets. Some were necessary, others were there to just complement the room.

One of the standout pieces that drew his attention was the tiny taxidermy reptile head that was situated on the side table next to the maroon couch.

"Interesting creature," Morgan said.

"I think it's an alligator, or maybe a crocodile. I'm no herpetologist," Yow chuckled.

"I think it's ugly," Dede said as she ran up and pointed at the thing.

"Ha. I wouldn't say ugly," Morgan laughed. "It's an intriguing specimen to say the very least."

"Good to know I'm not the only one who thinks so since I picked it out." Lilly smiled warmly at him.

Morgan blushed. "I used to play with salamanders growing up. Never anything too fierce."

"I love holding lizards," Lilly said with the vaguest hint of a seductive tone.

"Tell that to Dad," Yow interjected.

"Oh, quiet you," Lilly snapped at him. She then turned to Morgan. "You pay him no mind. He's nearly thirty yet he still acts juvenile. Would you believe around his own daughter too?"

Morgan could not help but erupt in laughter. "That's alright. I'm thirty-one and have the mind and restless body of a high schooler."

Lilly's smile broadened. "I'm glad to hear."

Yow was too busy making his way over to the phone to process what she had said. He saw that the red light was on indicating that there was a message left.

He hit the button on the answering machine. The monotone voice told him there was one missed message at 3:22 PM. Then, a familiar voice came on.

"Hello, Mr. Chung. This is your boss, Han Su. I regret to inform you that I need you to come in for the late shift. There has been an accident at one of the beaches. A few injured, one dead. Come in as soon as you can. In the meantime, I'll have the coroner look over the body."

Yow sighed and shook his head. "I wonder what could have happened at the beach to cause such a tragedy."

"Maybe it was a shark?" Sang stood next to him.

He shook his head, shooing off the idea of a killer fish in the area. "Probably some boating accident if I were to guess."

"Want me to come along?" Morgan asked.

"No. That's alright. Stay with the girls. I'll be back sometime in the morning." He turned to Sang. "Save me a plate of dinner please."

She nodded.

Soon, he was showered, dressed, and out the door.

Dede was not stressed about it too much. She was happy to see Morgan and figured they could all still have a good time regardless of her father's absence.

CHAPTER TWO

Livelihood.

The fisherman sat at the edge of the sandbank. On the surface of the murky water sat his bobber. He watched it intently, waiting for it to slip below the surface to signify a potential catch. It had been a good hour since he started his pleasureful activity and it was turning more into an aggravated one as the minutes ticked on.

There had not been a single nibble all morning. He had hoped the fishing would be good since the storm had passed leaving the ground muddy and full of insect activity. Mosquitoes coated the surface with a need to breed. Fish had plenty of options to pick from. Still, the water remained calm.

Not even a ripple.

Kenji Ho thought it was odd but chalked it up to being a fished-out section of the lagoon. As he sat in his canoe, he came to the conclusion that there were no fish there and reached for his paddle. As he made his way downstream, he came across a few children playing by the water's edge. They were climbing a nearby tree with a branch that stuck out over the swamp. They used it to leap from into the gross-looking water.

The kids were native to a nearby village. Kenji had never visited it. They seemed friendly and welcoming enough but he had become a recluse in his own canoe ever since the events that happened last year.

He had not only lost his entire family but his way of life too. Fishing in the mangroves was not the same as when sporting a rod and reel on the island of Habito.

It was almost too much to even watch the kids. Each one reminded him of what Hai would have been like had he had the chance to grow and experience. He bit his lip and pressed on, eventually finding a path that led to a dead end. It was a little cove in of itself, not much in terms of variety but it was spacious enough to fit a large vessel in. It would do just fine.

Tossing his line into the yellow-brown water, he sat back and tried to clear his mind. There was no time like the present. He rather enjoyed being alone most days. Still, that longing to be a father and husband crept into his subconscious. He often wondered if there would ever be an end to this torture he was experiencing.

Bloop.

A small, almost insignificant sound in the wall of jungle noise caught his ear. Kenji looked forward and saw that the bobber was still on the surface but there were ripples around it. Something had obviously nibbled on his bait. He reeled it in with a few cranks of his spool and watched as it dipped beneath the surface again. This time, it stayed down for a few seconds. Then it resurfaced.

Kenji remained motionless. The possibility of catching something had his eyes glued to the surface of the water. Then it happened again and again. *Is this damn fish going to take the bait or what?*

As if to answer him, the line suddenly shot out. It was dragged for nearly ten feet before Kenji secured the line. He then began to reel it in. The force of whatever was on the other end was immense. After a few tries, he realized he was not pulling the fish in but, rather, it was turning around, back towards him.

His palms began to get sweaty as did his brow. He did not have a free hand to wipe it so his perspiration dripped down his eyelid, some of it getting in his eyes. He squinted a bit but fought against the salty sting.

Then, an enormous displacement of water occurred. The surface was alive with ripples. It was as if something were cascading down an object.

Kenji relinquished his rod and quickly brushed the sweat off his face with his sleeve. Then, he looked closer at the animal. It was big, nearly ten feet. He could hardly believe what he was seeing. It was a shark. A bull shark, nevertheless.

Reaching for his spear that was attached to a rope, he waited for the fish to pass by. He then jabbed the shark atop its head and tied the rope around the body, securing it to the canoe.

"Damn nuisance." He cursed it as he started to paddle back upstream.

As he passed the area where the kids were playing, he realized they were all back on shore and running into the jungle, heading back to their home village.

***

Yow pulled up to the hospital. It was alive with a sea of reporters, scrambling to get updates on the beach injuries. He was thankful they did not recognize him as one of the doctors. It made it easy to slip inside undetected. Once in, he pulled on his lab coat and made his way down to the morgue.

Pat Crang stood over the body of a deceased bather. It was covered by a sheet. From the moment he saw Yow, his expression grew grim. "I don't think this was a boating accident."

"Come now, Pat. Don't be so quick to judge." Yow approached almost apprehensively. "We've seen plenty of boat fatalities. No two look the same."

"I'm having Shu from forensics look over the bodies this evening. She'll be able to detect any trace of metal."

"What if he didn't get hit by the propellor," Yow chuckled. "If he weren't, there wouldn't be a speck of residue."

"Then you explain to me how blunt force trauma from the bow or stern, or any side of the boat really, could explain how chewed up he looks," Pat inquired.

The two stood over the body tensely.

"Alright, let's get this over with." Yow lifted the sheet.

A ghastly sight indeed, the bather had clearly been mauled by some animal. His face was practically a hole with muscle barely holding it together. The flesh had been carved up but not by a blade. There were distinct, jagged marks. Further down, his belly was open, contents spilled somewhere in the ocean or down the gullet of whatever had killed him. His right arm was severed below the elbow and his chest had strange abrasions.

"Had to have been a shark." Pat noticed how Yow was examining the rashes. "Their skin is like sandpaper."

"This is almost too rough to be considered shark skin. There are pieces that were almost torn off. If it was a shark, the flesh would have been rubbed on at the very least," Yow explained.

He then strapped on some gloves and prodded at the bite marks. "These are from jagged teeth. Unless it was part dinosaur, I don't see how it could be a shark."

Pat observed closer. "He's sliced up. What other kind of animal could do this?"

Yow sighed and wiped his brow. "In all my years in this profession, I have never seen a body like this. I've seen shark attacks before. The absolute closest one I could compare this to is the bull shark. I'm only guessing because they stun their prey by bumping into it. It could explain some of these abrasions. Still, I'm skeptical."

"I'm not," a feminine voice could be heard from the doorway. "This was clearly a shark attack."

"What makes you say that, Shu?" Yow did not bother turning to face her.

"Because Kenji Ho just brought in a rather large specimen. A ten-foot bull shark. He found it on a river that connects directly to the beach where this boy was killed."

Yow shook his head. "Others were injured. Do they have statements?"

"They all say the same thing. The ocean seemed to come alive, and the water was rough going when they were attacked. It was impossible to see what attacked them for sure."

"Great," Yow sighed.

He then turned to Pat. "Feel like going for a walk?"

***

Down by the harbor he stood. He was not proud with achievement or showcasing any real glee. Kenji stood there with a blank expression next to the deceased shark. It had been strung up by a hook and pulley system against one of the pilings.

The dock was filled with onlookers and reporters alike. It made it near impossible for Sheriff Haruto Sans to navigate through. He had to turn on the squad car's siren to make any sort of progress. Once he managed to pull up a respectable walking distance from the parking lot to the pier, he got out. He showed his credentials to the guard and made his way towards the fisherman and his catch.

"Mornin'," Kenji looked to Haruto.

"My department says this fish has killed a person."

"My gut tells me it's possible. I haven't seen a bull this big in the area in a long time," Kenji retorted.

"Well, then on behalf of the Hong Kong Police Department, I want to thank you. To extend my gratitude, I want to issue you the reward money."

"I didn't know there was a reward?"

"It was about to be posted when news came that you killed the maneater."

Kenji nodded.

All the while, a commotion could be heard coming from where the guardsman stood.

"Let us through. We're from the hospital. We need to analyze the fish."

Haruto turned back and recognized Pat. He had seen him at the crime scene. "Let them through."

Yow, Pat, and Shu made their way into the harbor and onto the dock.

"That's one big smelly fish." Shu covered her nose with her sleeve.

"The odor wasn't as bad when it was alive," Kenji chuckled.

"I believe it," Shu stated.

Yow and Pat approached the fish. "May we?"

"Be my guests. I don't know what you're looking for but, whatever it is, I hope it helps with the investigation," Kenji smiled.

The examination was thorough yet despite this, Yow knew from the beginning it wasn't the culprit.

"May I borrow a knife?" he asked Kenji who happily obliged.

Without hesitation, Yow dug into the gums of the shark. No one objected. They knew it was one of the few ways to tell if a maneater was responsible for an attack. Soon, he produced the tooth.

"I'm always surprised how easy that is," Pat chuckled.

"You defang a lot of sharks?" Haruto asked, raising a brow.

"No, I've seen it done before though."

As the doctor and coroner studied the tooth, Shu approached Kenji. "Where exactly in the river did you find this specimen?"

"It was lurking in a little cove off the waterway a bit."

"I see." She made her way over to the sheriff next. "We should gut the shark. If its contents contain human remains, then the next logical step is to scout that area."

"Why?" he asked.

"Because, if this shark has killed a person and injured several others, there's no telling who else it may have attacked."

"You think it's a rogue?" Kenji asked.

Shu was taken aback a bit, surprised a local fishing bum knew what a rogue animal was. "I'd suspect so."

"What's a rogue?" Haruto inquired.

"Think of it as a fishy who doesn't act like a normal fishy," Kenji smirked.

"I don't think a gutting is quite necessary," Yow said.

"You think the tooth proves that the shark wasn't responsible?" Haruto wondered.

"That and the bite radius is too small," Pat began. "Our killer must have a huge mouth. I'm no marine biologist but, judging by the bite radius, it's got to have at least a four-foot span. At the very least."

"That's almost enough to fit a person inside!" Shu laughed. "A bit farfetched, don't ya think?"

"Maybe it wasn't a shark," Kenji said, gravely.

"Gator?" Haruto suggested.

The fisherman swallowed hard. "Crocodile."

"There hasn't been a croc attack around these parts for as long as I've been sheriff. Hell, probably longer."

"Doesn't mean they don't happen." Kenji turned and began down the dock.

Once he was out of ear reach, Shu looked to the sheriff. "What's eating him?"

"Kenji Ho came from a good village. One on Habito Island. One day, the entire community was taken out by a rogue wave. He swears up and down that a crocodile was responsible for not only the place's destruction, but the weather."

"He's just a drunkard," Pat stated.

"Still, let's not rule out a crocodile or even alligator for that matter. I want to get to the bottom of this and fast," Haruto ordered.

CHAPTER THREE

A happy existence.

Yow had returned home close to midnight. He made his way through the living room and towards the master bedroom. Sang was fast asleep as, he presumed, everyone else was. He quickly changed and climbed into bed next to her. She smelled so sweet as he cuddled up alongside her.

"Was it a boating accident?" she said suddenly.

He did not want to bring up the day's events too much. The idea of a hungry crocodile stalking the Mai Po River was scary enough. Furthermore, he did not want to ruin Morgan's vacation and the time they would all spend together.

On the other hand, he could not lie to her. He was never one to do so and was not about to start now. "We're not sure."

"Is the water safe?" she asked.

"Yes, dear. Everything is under control." He kissed the top of her forehead.

She was sweaty.

"Want me to turn on the fan?"

"No." She smiled. "I like it hot."

Looking up at him, she leaned forward and planted a kiss on his lips.

"What was that for?"

"No reason," Sang lied.

The night had been fun, with Lilly and Morgan getting along splendidly. Dede was as cute as ever. She felt happy, reassured that her life was one of beautiful existence. A warm swell of emotion came over her. One that she could hardly keep to herself.

"I love you, Dr. Chung."

"I love you, Mrs. Chung," Yow replied with a cool demeanor.

"Show me how much you love me, Doctor." She lifted the blankets, exposing herself to him.

He did not hesitate as he inched closer to her. The electrifying sexual tension between them grew and grew. Sang felt a release as he slid inside her. The rhythmic motion he performed gradually increased in speed.

Sang tried not to moan too loudly. She did not want Dede or the others to hear.

The room was now like a sauna. That did not stop either one of their lustful thrusts. It was not too long before Yow felt he was almost done. He was about to pull out.

"Don't." She reached out and pulled him closer by his shoulders. "Don't. I want to have another."

They had talked about it on and off a few months after Dede was born. Yow had been on the fence. Now, as he gazed at her amazing body, he did not have the heart to deny her request.

Unbeknownst to the lovers, there had been an audience. Lilly sat in one of the guest bedrooms listening intently. She was always grateful that her son had married someone so caring and full of life. It was clear she was not that bad in the sack either.

As the sounds of their moaning intensified, she began to think about her youth. She had been with many men in her glory days. Some were decent at the art of lovemaking, but the rest finished too early. She was always sought after for her looks.

The man she was now divorcing was older than her and cranky to no end. He was a rich oil tycoon who wanted someone who looked good at his side. He was not Yow's father. He had died shortly after their son was born.

She yearned for love. Not just the physicality of it, which was something she had not experienced in a great number of years, but in that solid connection between two people.

Morgan seemed nice but it was a pipedream. She often thought about him and his ogling of her. This time was different though. He seemed to be genuinely happy to see her. The thought made her smirk.

When Yow and Sang were done, she was still thinking of what it would be like to go at it with someone so young and well built like Morgan. She then realized it was inappropriate but that did not stop the wonders of it all. She figured she should talk with him and lay down the rules.

Morgan was in the living room, resting on the couch. He could not sleep with Yow and Sang's ceremony of love going on. He had tried to close his eyes and will the noises away.

He had not had a good interaction like that with someone in a long time. His last girlfriend turned out to be a conniving creep. She tried to ruin his career by claiming rape, but it all fell apart when the test results came back. They had not had sex yet. She was barking up the wrong tree as far as he was concerned.

That was four years ago. He had not been with anyone since. Not even a casual encounter. There was too much work to be done. Now that he had finally settled into his position, he felt he could start looking again.

There was a creaking sound as someone stepped on a weak floorboard in the hallway. He turned to see who it was. He hoped it was not Dede. She was too young to be hearing the sort of interactions her parents were having.

Instead, it was Lilly.

"Can't sleep?" she asked.

Morgan instantly blushed. Even with most of her make up off, besides some lipstick and a touch of eye-liner, she was still as beautiful as ever. She was wearing a satin, sky blue robe with pink flowers printed on it. Her hair was black as the night outside and had a nice wave to it. "No, you?"

She smiled. "No."

He could hardly contain himself.

"Want some company?" she asked.

"Sure." He beamed at her.

Lilly was surprised at how comfortable she felt with the idea of sitting next to him. It did not seem awkward at all. They were just conversing. Albeit it was going on one o' clock in the morning.

"Are you enjoying your stay so far?" she asked. Her voice was soft like an infant's tone. It was cutesy but had a sense of prowess to it.

"Yes. I'm finding it very easy to adjust to the totally different locale."

"That's good," she giggled.

"Yeah. Say, where did you get that taxidermy croc head?"

"Oh, that was down in a village on the Mai Po River. They have all sorts of cute trinkets and places to eat. It's very cultural, lots of tourists go there."

"Maybe I'd fit right in." He smiled.

"We should go." She caught herself suddenly. "I mean, we should all go for lunch."

Morgan did not miss a beat. "I'd like that."

She blushed a bit. "When you get to be my age, it's always a thrill to explore new places."

"Oh, you can't be that old. Regardless, it's never too late or too early to explore."

"Well, I'm fifty-eight so my time is limited."

"You're only as old as you feel." He did not seem phased by her age at all.

"Well, I feel good for being so old."

The two laughed. Then silence.

"I should get back to bed," she spoke with a hint of sadness.

"We'll all have fun tomorrow." He reached for her hand.

She did not resist as he planted a kiss on the top of it.

"Goodnight." He looked at her.

She really was gorgeous. Her firm cheekbones accentuated her shiny skin that was glistening in the moonlight that cast down into the room.

"Goodnight." She fought back her urges. Part of her wanted to take him. To let him do whatever he wanted to her. The kiss on the hand was sweet but she wanted more. She fought the urge and stood up.

Morgan watched her as she made her way back to her room. She seemed to be floating as if she was atop clouds, although he chalked it up to her graceful stride.

***

Kenji sat in his boathouse with a bottle of alcohol in one hand and a cigar in the other. He had watched Yow and Pat dissect the shark only to find a can of tonic, some fish parts, and even a chunk of rubber from a deflated car tire. There were no signs of human remains.

He had not received the award money but was honored with admiration for stopping a potential maneater. He chuckled as he thought back on it. There was no evidence to support the idea of it being a rogue, let alone killing anyone. It was just a fish caught in the wrong place at the wrong time.

There was nothing else he thought could have killed that man and injured those bathers. It had to have been a crocodile. He wondered if it was the same one he had seen destroy his home in Habito. Time and time again he had scrutinized the mental image of the beast. *Was it really that big? Did I suddenly have an active imagination? Did the storm come from it?* They were all questions he knew he did not have the answers for yet.

If it was the same animal, that meant it was still out there and could be liable to do some serious damage.

Taking a swig of the last of his booze, he stood up and flicked the cigar out the window and into the water below. He then managed to make his way up the stairs and into the loft where his hammock was calling him. He knew he would be in for another restless night.

It was the morning sun that cast down through the cracks in the ceiling that made him awaken in annoyance. He usually slept on his right side but had lately taken a liking to the left. It came at a cost because the sun was now not hitting his back but directly on his face. He swung his legs over the side of his suspended bed and hopped off.

Stretched and relaxed, he made his way back downstairs where he saw something discerning. On the ground in front of where he had sat the night before was the remnants of the cigar as well as a large burn mark that surrounded it.

He began to wonder how the whole place had not burnt to the ground. The fire seemed to have started only to have been put out shortly after. The stench of burnt wood surrounded him.

It did not rain last night nor was there any heavy winds. Kenji looked down at the floor and then up towards the ceiling, seeing past it in his head. He inwardly thanked Dala. "At least someone's looking out for me."

Reaching down, he picked up the cigar and, this time, he made sure it went out the window and into the sea. He then walked down to his canoe and prepared it for the morning routine of fishing. Although, this time, a certain spot called to him. The Mai Po River was holding secrets that he needed confirmation on. There was no other way around it, he had to get to the bottom of it all. Perhaps he could even put an end to the beast that tore his family and home away from him.

He walked back up the dock and went into his shed. Then, with determination driving him, he hefted a miniature engine and brought it down towards his second vessel, a small speedboat. After a few minutes, he had it situated on the stern and drove out onto the ocean.

It was not long before he found the location he was looking for. The inlet led to a saltwater river then went for miles. Vegetation grew thick in the area. There were even some low hanging trees with branches and leaves practically touching the water's surface. It was a damp, humid place. Everything felt miserable there. As soon as he left the open ocean and entered the river, he began to feel uneasy. It was not like last time where he felt in control with a fishing rod in hand and a hook in the other.

One of the compartments held something he hoped stood a chance against a crocodile as worthy of fear and respect. There was no guarantee it was the same crocodile, but Kenji knew it would be cathartic for him, nevertheless.

CHAPTER FOUR

A new awakening.

Something felt different as Sang rose from her bed. It was as if the new dawn was bestowing her a chance at an even better life. She carefully pulled the covers off her naked body, and she gently placed her feet delicately on the carpet floor. Then, with the grace of a ballerina she walked over to one of the tables situated between their closet and one of the two windows in the room.

Uncovering the casing of the record player, she let it fall back against the wall without so much as a thud. She then knelt down and fingered through the records. Eventually, she fished out one from an American band, The Carpenters. She turned the album around to side B and placed it on the platform. Then, with a careful placement of the diamond needle, the song *Superstar* began to play.

Yow turned slightly at the sound of the harp being strummed. As the intro to the ballad began to play out, he finished looking over his shoulder and was now facing Sang as she danced in the morning light that beamed through the window.

Her completely naked body glistened as she swayed her hips and rolled her head from side to side. It bobbed when she could stretch it more and then slowly moved to the opposite side. She looked so content and at peace that Yow rested his head in his hand as his elbow pushed into the mattress. He observed her majestic motions as if she were taking the dance seriously. It was all feeling that was further proven by her occasional smirks that broke the illusion that it was some intense act.

When the chorus hit, she led her hands to her head and placed them on either side. She was exposing herself to him fully. Her bush was full and ready for exploration. She could not help but part her legs slightly with the sound of the beat.

"Didn't I give you enough last night?"

She barely shook her head, but it was clear enough she wanted more. She seemed so happy. He was so lucky. She was not only dancing for him though. It was the rhythm that guided her. She felt the surge of emotion as the second surge powered through her, essentially giving her a super charge.

He got up. Having forgotten his nude state, he made his way towards her. She reached out and placed her hands on his face.

"Thank god we have locks on the door."

Sang smiled and guided her hand lower until she had his manhood in her firm grip. She then lowered herself and began to pleasure him. It was a long, hard process but she did not show signs of fatigue. She was vigorous but not violent. She knew how he liked it.

It concluded with no trace of the substance spilling anywhere in the room. She stood up and walked into the bathroom to freshen up as Yow collapsed on the bed. He seemed to be more tired than her.

Regardless of the attempted silence of the act, Lilly had caught an earful of it as she walked by their room. She began to scorn herself for last night. She had the chance to have that same sort of satisfaction with Morgan last night.

Still, she knew it was not time yet. She was trying to play hard to get but it was not as easy with him. For some reason, he made her feel differently than any man before. He was handsome yet had an innocent little boy side to him that seemed as though he was inexperienced. Somehow, she did not think it was that and wondered if he was just nervous around her because he felt the same way she did.

A door opened across the hall and Dede came strolling out. "Good morning, Grandma."

"Good morning, deary." She smiled at her.

"What's for breakfast?"

"How about I whip us up some French toast?"

"Yummy!" Dede cheered.

Lilly held out her hand and guided Dede out into the kitchen. Morgan was still on the couch in the den, as sleepy as a sloth, complete with one arm laying lazily off the side.

He even sleeps peacefully. Lilly observed him for perhaps a second too long. Morgan stirred but did not open his eyes.

"You coming, Grandma?"

"Yes, let's make some breakfast!" She smiled.

An hour later and everyone was situated around the table.

"This is excellent food, Ms. Chung," Morgan smiled.

Lilly grinned. "It was nothing."

"I've got a big day planned for us!" Yow said, excitedly. "It's mostly going to be on the beach, but I think, later, we can go on the boardwalk and enjoy the sunset."

"Sounds lovely." Sang placed a hand on her husband's lap.

"I've got a new camera," Yow beamed.

"Really!" Dede exclaimed. "Will it take good pictures like the last one?"

"Even better ones!" Yow smiled.

"Hurray!" she cheered in response.

"Let's get ready in a few minutes and leave the house by oh say quarter of eight?"

"Sounds good to me," Morgan smiled.

"I'll have to try on my new bathing suit." Lilly could not help but glance at Morgan.

"Oh! The black one?" Sang inquired.

"Yep! I'll be a knockout granny on the beach!" she laughed.

"Who's going to knock you out?" Dede asked.

"It's a figure of speech, deary." Lilly patted her head gently.

"You guys say that all the time. I don't even know what a figure of speech is."

The adults laughed.

***

Puttering down the river on his makeshift speedboat, Kenji perused the waterlines as if shopping for a new pet. He was not sure what animal he would get but he would make sure to take care of it. In this case, he would put it down for good and mount it on his wall.

As he entered the swampier section, he saw the water turned from a clear blue to a murky brown as he made his way further in. He could practically sense it, the elusive carnivore watching him from the reeds.

There was no clear sign of a crocodile being in the area. No mud had been pushed up on the banks nor any carcasses lying about. Still, the aura of death permeated the sweltering spot. The topography looked sad as if weeping deep sorrows from the intense humidity. They hung low enough to practically touch the water.

Flora or fauna aside, the area seemed to harness some sort of energy. It wasn't a presence so much as a paranormal vibe. It was as if something was there and did not want him around. Yet he continued to prod around with his paddle, attempting to irritate anything on the surface by slapping the water. He knew it would not only cause annoyed animals to retreat into the depths but also attract certain ones.

It happened then. The oar hit something solid. Kenji froze in place. The vibration that ran through the pole registered it as not being a flat surface. It was rather bumpy. As he pulled it back, it kept hitting little divots within the object. It was scaly no doubt. By the feel of it, it would have had to have horns, or indents.

A tail.

Kenji slowly raised the paddle towards him and then stood up and held it aloft.

Even though he knew the beast was there, he could not see it. There was too many algae and seaweed on the surface to see his own reflection, let alone a massive reptile. Suddenly, ripples began to form in the once placid waters. They came up everywhere, surrounding him and the entire vicinity of the river. Kenji looked around and realized he was in a cove off to the side.

"I found your home," he snarled.

Something shifted under the water. He could only catch brief glimpses of the enormous killer as it glided under him. It did not surface though. Instead, it continued to press forward out of the cove and into the river.

He stood there in silence. Listening, waiting for it to strike. It never did. Then, he heard something that terrified him even more. Laughter and cheers. They sounded young and youthful. Full of life which was something the crocodile would take away.

"No!" His face turned pale.

Quickly sitting down, he tugged on the cord to start the engine.

Nothing.

"What the!"

He pulled again and again until it finally came to life. By that time, the ripples ahead had disappeared. He had no idea where it went visually but knew where it was heading.

***

Tang laughed heartily as Ro held onto the tree limb for dear life. He was having trouble finding the courage to take that plunge into the water. His brother, Koto, was trying not to laugh but found it hard. The very sight of his younger sibling clutching the branch as if it was their mother was too much.

Ro had always been skittish but never this bad.

"Just let go!" Koto said between a chuckle.

"I can't!" Ro cried out.

"What's the matter? Afraid the swamp monster's going to get you?" Tang bellowed.

"Ro, I'm in here. There's nothing dangerous in this part of the river," Koto explained, trying to reassure him that it was safe.

"What if something comes from another part of the river?" Ro cried.

Koto had to admit that that was a fair point. Still, he had to get him in the water. He did not want to be known as the villager with the coward for a brother.

"Please, little brother. Get in. Do it for me." He was practically pleading.

"You just don't want to look like a loser in front of your friends!" Ro began to cry.

Koto had to admit, Ro was smart. Smarter than he was at that age. It seemed like a lifetime ago when he was seven when, in reality, it had only been five years.

"C'mon, ya big baby! I want a turn!" Tang said, annoyed now. "If you're too scared to hang with the cool kids then maybe you should..." He paused.

"What?" Koto looked at him funny.

"Did you see that?" Tang took a step forward towards the water.

Koto turned to looked around but did not see anything in there with him.

"Nice try," he laughed.

"I mean it. There's something in the water!"

"What?" Ro stammered, his lip pouting.

"It's... Oh wow! That's so cool!"

"What is?" Koto was not amused.

"It's a popular kid running in after a loser!" Tang charged suddenly into the water, causing a splash that sprayed Koto in the face and Ro in the back.

"Raw! I'm the cool crocodile coming to get you!" Tang laughed.

"Ha! Well I'm a groovy gator coming to fight you!" Koto lunged forward and the two began to wrestle.

Ro watched as the two had a good time in the muddy water. He began to feel left out. The feeling of regret came over him as quickly as the massive pair of jaws that appeared from seemingly out of nowhere and engulfed Koto and Tang in one bite.

At first, he did not know what to make of it. He thought it had to be another joke. An elaborate prank but a prank, nevertheless. They must have constructed a massive crocodile head out of clay and chicken wire. He had done something similar in an art session, but he had made a snake that was a fraction of the size.

He snapped out of it when the water began to turn red.

"Koto!" he cried out.

The crocodile was still on the surface. It did not see him at first until he screamed. Following this, its head rose and looked up. Ro froze in place.

He began to mumble about how he would be a good boy and not get in any trouble. He would make his parents proud and even his brother. Koto was not there anymore though. The crocodile was.

It lowered its head into the water to gain traction. It then shot upward. Ro could only watch as the hideous pair of jaws that claimed Koto and Tang raced towards him.

Crack.

Kenji saw the crocodile for the first time in a year. There was no doubt it was the same one. It was clinging onto a tree branch which clearly could not sustain the weight of the beast.

The branch snapped and fell into the water. Kenji swore he could hear muffled screaming coming from within its mouth.

"No!" he screamed.

He then directed the boat towards the crocodile and sped towards it, aiming to ram it and finish the monster off for good. It suddenly turned and faced him. The yellowish orange eyes locked onto him. They looked like eons of death and decay. As if this particular crocodile had been around for centuries, only now deciding to wreak havoc.

Suddenly afraid, he turned the boat and made his way down the river, in the opposite direction. Anything to put distance between himself and the crocodile.

CHAPTER FIVE

Hot coals of hell.

Last year in 1976, the June month had been sweltering. The trees looked sad, and the water levels were low in certain areas, especially in the rivers and streams. Everyone complained.

Now it was almost unbearable, pushing one hundred degrees with a higher level of humidity than previously encountered in recent times. The unmatched weather was driving most of the citizens of Hong Kong mad, namely in the district of Kowloon. The Chung family resided there and were among the very few that did not mind.

Sang prepared herself and Dede for a fun day at the beach. She donned a skimpier yellow two-piece string bikini while her daughter wore a conservative one piece. Yow was in the next room over with Morgan as they put on their swimwear.

"You're definitely turning into a dad." Morgan laughed at Yow's wardrobe. He was wearing a white t-shirt, red swim trunks and his thickest set of black frame glasses.

"I still can't believe what you're wearing is allowed out in public," Yow remarked, looking at Morgan in his tight black speedo. "You better not lose those or see a pretty girl. Both scenarios would be embarrassing."

"Not the latter, my friend." Morgan patted him on the shoulder. "Say, where's Lilly?"

"She's already down at the beach. She got ready early."

"Alright then, let's not keep your mom waiting."

"Let me just check in on Sang and Dede." Yow went over to their room and knocked on the door. "We're almost ready," Sang said, cheerfully.

"Okay. I'm just going to grab my camera and then we'll meet you two outside," Yow said.

"Okay, honey," Sang replied.

Yow walked over to the tabletop near the door and grabbed his small camera.

"That must have cost you a pretty penny." Morgan came up behind him.

"You bet. Thing's waterproof too."

"Impressive."

The two laughed and made their way out the door and to the car. When Morgan climbed in, he nearly hopped back out.

"Ow!" he exclaimed.

"What's wrong?"

"My ass just got roasted on your seat."

Yow bellowed with laughter.

"I hope I didn't get burnt." Morgan fought the urge not to smirk but was losing.

"I'll get a towel." Yow trudged back inside just as Sang and Dede stepped out.

"What's the matter?" Sang asked.

"Doctor hot butt over there didn't think to place a towel down on the seat," Yow explained.

Sang blushed with amusement.

It took roughly twenty minutes to get to Repulse Bay Beach from the Chung estate and Morgan was feeling better already. He could hardly contain himself as he wondered what Lilly was wearing. He had been interested in how she looked for being so much older and having had a child. He expected wrinkles and body fat in places that would be unappealing to most. To him though, that did not matter. He was beginning to enjoy just how sweet and courteous she was. He wanted to get to know her for more than just her body.

Pulling into the parking lot, Sang helped Dede out of her driver's seat while Yow and Morgan grabbed some towels. The sun beat down on them as if they were in an oven and the temperature was rising.

"I can't wait to get in the water." Morgan wiped his brow.

"It's not too bad out. Still, I know what you mean. It's refreshing," Yow explained.

"Your family is built different I swear," Morgan laughed.

Sang and Dede came around the front of the car and the four made their way onto the beach. It was packed with people. The sea was covered in carefully spaced boats and jet skis. There were three lifeguard towers and one patrol officer that Yow did not remember the name of.

As they made their way onto the beach, they passed a concession stand. Dede got a whiff of grilled hotdogs with a hint of relish being applied to them. "What's for lunch?"

"Your mother packed some cheese and crackers," Yow explained.

"I want a hotdog!" Dede exclaimed.

"Maybe later," Sang smiled at her.

"Okay, Mommy," she replied while showing signs of giddiness.

"Look, there's Grandma!" Yow told Dede.

Morgan spotted her last and, when he did, he was dumbstruck. She was wearing a red one-piece halter swimsuit and donning a pair of sunglasses and a white beach hat. She was not overly exposing herself, but it was clear she was showing the parts that attracted most men. Morgan fought with every ounce of mindpower to keep himself from becoming erect.

"Hey, sweetie!" Lilly called to her granddaughter.

Dede scurried towards her, nearly tripping on the sand.

"Careful, deary!" she called to her.

Dede quickly closed the gap between them and gave her a hug and a peck on the cheek.

"Let's have fun!" Lilly told her, quickly standing up and making her way towards the waterline.

Yow and Sang set up the beach towel while Morgan placed the basket of cheese and crackers down. The three then began to settle in.

Sang reached into the basket and pulled out a bottle of lotion. Reaching behind her, she placed it in the waiting hands of Yow. He got to work quick. At first, he was rough, but she did not mind. She knew that he would soon be gentler as he caressed her shoulder blades.

Morgan watched Lilly who was standing on the shore while Dede played in the water. Even from behind, Lilly was a specimen. Nothing on her was noticeably saggy. She could pass for being in her early thirties. There was an aged experience about her, as though she possessed a strong sense of understanding on how to make herself happy.

Dede began to splash around, causing seawater to slosh and spray everywhere. "Grandma, watch this!"

She ducked beneath the surf and placed her palms on the sandy bottom. Then, with minimal effort, she shot her feet upward, completing a handstand. She then resurfaced and looked to see her grandma clapping.

"That was nice, deary!"

Morgan got up off the towel and made his way towards the water. Sang watched him and smiled. She hoped he and Lilly would get together soon. It was time she had a man in her life that was not a piece of turd. Yow did not pay too much attention to his friend, assuming he was going for a swim.

Lilly stood rigid, as if she could feel his presence nearby. She began to blush and tried her best not to smile.

"How's the water?" Morgan asked her.

"It's perfect. Feels great rushing past your toes," she said to him.

"Sounds amazing!" Morgan walked past her and into the sea.

He was being subtle. She knew he wanted her to follow but she could not find the courage. Not in front of her son. She watched Morgan as he began to backstroke. He bobbed up and down in the surf. The speedo was pressed so tightly around his groin she could see the outline of his manhood.

She returned her focus to Dede who was a bit further out now.

"Don't go too far out, honey," she called to her.

Plowing through the water with incredible speed, it was charging across the bay as if there was nothing around it. A presence all on its own. There was no intention of slowing down. Now until it felt solid ground.

Those kids were mere appetizers. The main course was bound to happen like an impending doom. It was going to happen again, and nothing could stop it.

"Look out!" Lilly screamed suddenly at the sight of the speedboat slicing through the water. It was going so fast that she almost did not see it until it was hugging the shoreline.

Morgan heard her scream and looked in her line-of-view. The watercraft was closing the gap between it and Dede. He did not have time to think, instead charging towards the little girl. He brought his arms up and down, pounding them into the surf.

Dede, none the wiser, continued to play. She was about to go under again when she felt a pair of strong hands pull her back up. She was then yanked to the left and pulled alongside a hairy chest.

By the time they were ashore, Yow and Sang were showering her with hugs and kisses. Lilly ran over and did the same. She then stood up and hugged Morgan.

"Thank you!"

"Don't mention it," he said between deep breaths. His lungs were burning. He could not tell if it was from the adrenaline wearing off or his love for Lilly growing.

Yow stood up and looked at the boat as it began to shrink as it drove further away. "That's Kenji Ho's boat."

"You know him?" Sang shouted.

"You could say that." Yow returned his attention to Dede. "Are you alright, honey?"

Dede nodded. She was clearly shaken but not too severely. "Can we go home?"

"Yes," Yow stated. "I have a few phone calls to make anyway."

Kenji sped across the bay area until he found the nearest dock close to the sheriff's department. He pulled into a slick, a wave of adrenaline still coursing through him. He could feel cold beads of sweat pouring down his face and it was not just because of the humidity. He made his way towards the steps that led to the sidewalk.

He was downtown now. No more than two blocks from his destination. His feet guided him with tremendous agility and grace as he sprinted. He was thankful he was still fit and capable of running for great distances without tiring.

When he saw the sign with the letters *Kowloon Sheriff's Department* labeled on them, he breathed a sigh of relief, allowing a great weight to lift off his shoulders. He wasted no time running inside and to the secretary's desk.

"I need to speak with Haruto!" he shouted.

Before the secretary could answer, a man of familiar frame and stature appeared in the doorway. "I'd like to speak with you too."

"Sheriff!" Kenji exclaimed. "We need to close the beaches and alert the   coast   guard   now!"

"What's this I hear about you speeding across the bay?" Haruto ignored Kenji's pleas.

"That's not important."

"Really? You nearly, and I mean by a hair, ran over a little girl. Yow Chung's little girl to be precise."

Kenji's face turned pale. "I didn't even see her."

"Were you drinking?" Haruto asked.

"No. There are more pressing matters at hand though."

Haruto did not want to listen to the ravings of the man who was the only survivor of a tropical storm. This was not the first time he had tried to prosper from tragedy.

"Then how could you not see her or Yow's friend as he pulled her out of the way?"

"Because I needed to get here and had tunnel vision on, I guess."

"Tunnel vision?"

Kenji sighed. He was getting tired of conversing about something that left no one deceased or even injured.

He took an enormous breath and began. "I was on the Mai Po River, trying to hunt down the predator that attacked those bathers. I saw it. I saw the damn thing that tore my home and people to shreds. Not only that, I saw it kill some village kids."

"Kids? Predator? What are you talking about?"

"The crocodile!" Kenji cried."A crocodile on the Mai Po River just killed some village kids?" Haruto inquired.

"At least one. I heard multiple voices earlier before," Kenji confirmed.

"Then what?"

"I drove out of there. I came directly here. I'm sorry if I almost injured a kid but there are going to be a lot more dead kids if we don't do something quick!"

Haruto was relieved that the waiting room was empty and that most of the other officers were on duty. The story was almost too ridiculous to believe. It was not impossible, but it was uncommon.

"Come into my office." He opened the door and Kenji stormed in.

CHAPTER SIX

The concept of youth.

Lilly Chung had lived a fulfilled adult life. She had married, had a brilliant little boy, and was a cheerful person to be around. She was not always happy though.

As the living room took in the evening sky, creating a bright yellow glow against the walls, she sat on a leather recliner as Dede played with her dolls. She saw her granddaughter pull at one of the figure's hairs and did a playful soft scream. Lilly found it adorable, as did Sang who was lying on the couch.

The shock of what happened today still had not worn off. She was thankful there was no accident, but it was almost too close to one to bear. The sense of how short life could be washed over her like a mighty wave. Dede was only seven and a half years old. She could have had her whole existence erased before she even had a chance to do anything with it. The very thought chilled Sang to her core.

Yow had noticed how pale Sang looked. "You alright, honey?"

"Yes. Just tired is all."

"Maybe we should go to bed early?" Yow told her.

"I want to stay up and play!" Dede whined.

"We have a fun day planned for tomorrow. Besides, Morgan's already in bed. I'm sure you'll want to wake up before him so you can make his breakfast," Yow smiled.

"You mean it?" She was ecstatic.

"Most definitely!" Yow told her.

Sang got up. "Okay then, let's all go to bed. We have breakfast in the morning, so we need to get some much-needed rest."

Dede cheered and followed her mom as she was led to her own room. She returned to see that Yow was still sitting on the couch. "You ready, honey?"

"Yeah. You going to bed too, Mom?" He turned to Lilly.

"I think I'll stay up for a bit. Going to enjoy the night sounds until I drift off."

"It is a peaceful night." Yow smiled and then went with his wife to their bedroom.

Lilly sat in silence, appreciating the crickets stridulating and the occasional owl hoot. She loved when the Collard Scops showed up. Whenever she could see them outside they looked angry but seemed curious. They were always too adorable not to admire.

An hour passed and she began to get heavy eyed. She thought about the idea of going for a swim in the pool but did not want to wake anyone up. Besides that, she did not believe Morgan would come out to talk to her. She knew he was taking things slow, testing the waters. She could wait.

Sang lay wide awake in the bed. Yow was still reading a magazine with the lamp on but was slowly succumbing to sleep. She wondered how anyone could read when tired. She would have to stop every few words just to go back and reread them.

There was more on her mind though.

"I'm scared," Sang said suddenly.

Yow put the catalogue down and turned to her. "What's wrong?"

She took a deep breath. "What happened today. It could have been horrible. I can't fathom what it would be like to lose Dede, let alone at such a young age."

"You mustn't worry about things that did not happen. You're borrowing trouble."

"I know. I know. I still think about it. I just can't help it."

He reached for her, and she shuffled closer to him. "Just be thankful. She's alive, Morgan saved her. I talked with the sheriff, and he said he'll have a talk with Kenji Ho. I'm sure it was all just one big misunderstanding. He probably didn't see her."

"Are you on his side now?" Sang asked.

"No. I talked with him once. He seemed like a nice guy. Understanding and all there."

"Then what happened? Why did he almost kill our daughter?"

"I don't know. I'll be in touch with the sheriff tomorrow after breakfast. I'm sure he'll have an explanation at the very least."

He kissed the top of her head. "I love you. I would never let anything happen to you or Dede."

"We should keep an eye on her. Your mother should have been in the water with her."

"She was standing there, watching her. She probably didn't see the boat until it was almost too late."

Sang thought about Lilly and Morgan. Around the same time he went into the water, she turned her attention towards him. She could not be certain, but she found it likely. Still, she did not want to make a tense situation even more awkward, so she dropped it.

"I guess you're right."

He kissed her head again and then reached over and turned off the lamp. The hours passed but neither of them fell asleep. They were deep in thought until around three in the morning when the fatigue won, and the night claimed them.

***

Sheriff Haruto Sans could not believe what he was told. A crocodile that size could destroy an entire village as if it were a toy. Kenji had described it as being thirty meters long and that it could conjure up bad weather. It was impossible, too fantastic. There was no doubt in his mind that Kenji was bringing up the past and misremembering it.

Three kids were reported missing in a village near the Mai Po River but there were no bodies. Just a case number to put into the file of missing persons reports. First the bather that was killed and now these kids. He could not decipher which was worse, the missing kids or the wild stories Kenji told him about what happened.

Definitely the missing kids.

He reassured himself that if the kids were killed by a crocodile that it would make headlines no doubt. Regardless, he was going to the Mai Po River at some point to look into Kenji's claim. He had told him that it knocked down some trees and took one of the children with it. He would have to recruit Pat and Shu. That much he knew.

At quarter of four in the morning, he left the office and drove home. Thoughts of kids being eaten by a reptile clouded his mind. It would have been horrible to experience, especially for a child.

The glow of the neon lights were less blinding than before midnight. Around this time, shops and clubs were closing and people were going home. Haruto would go home, sleep for an hour, and come back to the station after grabbing a bite at a diner.

It was going to be a crazy week, he could feel it in his bones.

***

Kenji sat in his bungalow with a bottle hanging loosely from his hand. He had visions of the past passing before his eyes even when they were closed. His eyelids were like movie screens and his eyes the projectors. He saw his family taken from him in a gust of wind. He then witnessed the tree snapping and the screams of a boy echoing across the river until they were muffled by the murky water.

Lightning flashed continuously in his vision. What showed between them was one possible future. One where Dala was cradling Hai while he prepared breakfast with the frying pan near the fireplace. Everyone was so happy. He was content living on Habito now, unlike before.

For the first time in a year, Kenji smiled with a level of peace and happiness he had not experienced once during that time. He felt like he was in his own paradise. Habito was his utopia and his family, his home.

He turned to give his family the meal when another flash of lightning occurred. When his vision recovered, he saw Dala. She had been mutilated and physically destroyed. Her insides were her outsides and her beautiful face was nothing but mush. Kenji screamed but stopped short when he heard Hai crying somewhere off in the distance. He ran outside to find him.

"Hai!" he called out while asleep.

The baby's crying grew more distant. Despite this, he kept trying to run towards him. Every time he thought he successfully closed the gap, it was all for nothing because he kept getting further and further away.

"Come back!" He was crying now.

Another flash of lightning stopped him in his tracks. What stood before him was the beast. The mighty crocodile. A hundred feet long and ready to destroy. It roared and Kenji screamed in defiance.

He then shot up in his cot, bathed in sweat and hyperventilating. Placing his hands on his face, he sat there weeping. The morning sun was just coming through the cracks in the ceiling as he lamented on what happened.

"Where did you go, Hai?" he wondered.

***

Lilly rose from her bed in bliss. She felt relaxed as if the previous night's peaceful serenity stayed with her in her sleep. She stretched her arms and then swung her legs over the side of the bed. They touched down on her light pink satin slippers with the matching fluffy poof on the top. After she went to the bathroom to wash her face and apply a touch of makeup, she exited her room.

She began to wonder why the house was so quiet. She did not hear the sounds of Dede playing or clanking of dishes as she and her parents prepared dishes. When she entered the den, she found it empty. The kitchen was pristine as if it had not been touched all night.

Looking over at the clock on the wall, she saw that it was eight on the dot. It had been half an hour since she woke up and not a sound could be heard.

You'll want to wake up before him so you can make his breakfast. The sentence went through Lilly's mind. Yow had told Dede the plan last night. Morgan would not be asleep much longer, she assumed. She began to worry.

"Hello?" she called out softly.

"Good morning," Morgan said from behind her in the hallway.

"Oh. I wasn't sure if anyone was here."

"They didn't mention anything to me about leaving first thing," he told her. "My guess is they're still asleep."

Just then the door creaked open behind him and Dede came walking out of her room. She rubbed her eyes and looked blankly at them. "Where's Mommy and Daddy?"

"They must still be asleep," Morgan suggested to her.

"They went to bed early though," Dede told him.

Morgan gently scooted past her and over to their room. He softly knocked on the door and opened it a couple of inches. "Yow. Hey man. Are you awake?"

There was a groan before he answered. "What time is it?"

"A little after eight."

"Man, I did not sleep well."

"Me neither." Sang was clinging to him.

Dede appeared by Morgan's side. "What about breakfast?"

"Aw, honey," Yow sighed. "How about you and Grandma take Morgan out to eat. Remember the little restaurant around the corner. The one with the ball pit."

"Yes!" She became excited about the idea of hopping in the play pen they had there.

"Well, have Grandma take you and Morgan there. Maybe we'll be there shortly too. We just need to sleep a bit longer."

"We can wait for you," Morgan suggested.

"No. Have a good time," Sang told him. She knew it may be the only chance Morgan and Lilly would have to be alone. There was plenty she could do to keep Yow here for the morning.

"If you insist," Morgan told her as he gently closed the door.

Dede ran up to Lilly. "We're going to Kans!"

CHAPTER SEVEN

On the fence.

At odds with one another, Kenji Ho and Haruto Sans paddled down the river in the canoe. Kenji had left the portable engine back at his shack and was kicking himself for it ever since. What he did not have in speed he made up for with firepower. At his feet was a case of dynamite, complete with fuses. He had instructed Haruto to have two lighters on him in case he lost one or one got wet.

Haruto was partially doubtful of Kenji's story with the kids and in even more of a disbelief on what he saw on Habito Island. There was no way such a monster could exist. Maybe in some Chinese legend there was a beast of such magnitude. Those old tales were outdated as far as he was concerned. He was certain about one thing though. There was nothing supernatural happening in Kowloon or in all of Hong Kong. It was all fake.

"You know the world has outgrown magic and hocus pocus stuff," he said suddenly.

Kenji sighed. "On Habito, we had a saying. Out like the morning sun, the rays stretch and fade away."

"Meaning?"

"We're fading away as a culture. It's 1977 and the times are changing."

"Don't they always?" Haruto asked.

"Not this drastically. A cataclysmic event would have had to occur any time prior to the twentieth century. Like the forming of life or the extinction of the dinosaurs."

"Yeah, yeah. Anyway. Speaking of dinosaurs. Where's yours?" Haruto joked.

"We're near Deep Bay. The inlet should be coming up."

They continued to paddle. Haruto's eyes periodically became attached to the bright greenery all around. The brown water was a strange contrast. It made the whole area seem drab and bleak despite the pleasant vegetation.

Kenji lowered his paddle deeper until it touched the bottom. He then shifted it to the right so the boat would turn left. It then inched further into an inlet.

"We're here," he stated.

For some reason, unbeknownst to him, Haruto suddenly became tense. The overhang of tree limbs and their lush leaves did not seem so inviting anymore. It felt like he was in a domain of something beyond his control and that he could not protect himself from whatever was to come.

"Look!" Kenji shouted suddenly.

He made Haruto nearly jump out of his skin. *"What!"*

The sharpness in the sheriff's voice concerned Kenji. "Sorry, did I scare you?"

"Kinda."

"Well, sorry. But look at the sandbank."

Haruto caught his breath and then looked at it. There was indeed a large impression. It appeared as if a pavement roller had flattened it out in a large indent. The way it was situated though, the truck would have fallen into the water.

"That was where its tail was at one point."

The dinghy bumped into the sandbank and Haruto jumped again.

"Stop startling me!"

"Sorry," Kenji said as he climbed out and began to walk up the steep hill.

Haruto fished out his service revolver when Kenji shouted, "Hey! Look   at   this!"

The urgency in his voice made the sheriff leap to his feet and bound the dune in a few long strides. He then bumped into Kenji as the two fell to the mushy earth below. He looked down at his uniform.

"Shit! I just had this washed and dried this morning."

Kenji stared blankly at the ground. "I think you're going to need Pat and   Shu   to   come   out   here.   Pronto."

"Why?" he asked.

The fisherman pointed to the ground, and he followed the line of view.

There, on the ground, was a round hole. Haruto looked closer and realized there were triangular sections at the top.

"Is that what I think it is?"

"Yes, Sheriff. That is the footprint of my nightmares."

***

In Yuen Long, over one hundred cattle were kept on a farm. They provided the milk for the Kowloon Dairy Company. The process was meticulous and slow but rewarding, nevertheless. The supplier was renowned for their high-quality product. There had been reviews in columns praising not only the delicacy, but the rewarding experience retailers had working with them. The workers on the other hand had different kinds of experiences.

On a good day, twenty workers would be in place. Cows would be milked for the creamy contents in the udders and placed into bottles and barrels to be driven to Kowloon. It was a fifteen-minute drive to the facility where the product was distributed. As well as only twenty minutes from the Mai Po River.

Yuto, the associate manager, stood on a walkway that was above the worker area. There were rails on each side, which he held with both hands as he crossed. He was deathly afraid of heights, but he had to get to Chen's office and fast.

Boss Chen was currently working on the outline for his quarterly report when Yuto came barging in.

"Can you believe this!" Chen shouted.

"Boss, I think there's something you..."

"I'll tell you there's something. They want 2,000 yuan to keep the ACs on the salesfloor and freezers. Last year, at this time, it was 1,500!"

Yuto was gasping for air. He had just run halfway across the grounds and into the facility to present news to Chen and was now having trouble breathing.

"You should lay off the fast food, Yuto. You're going to have a heart attack one of these days."

Hatata suddenly came walking into the room. He was one of the security officers who was even more out of shape than Yuto. Chen realized immediately that the two ran a long way to get here to tell him something. *Who am I kidding, it couldn't have been that far.*

"There..." Yuto's voice was hoarse as if he had smoked all his life.

"What the hell is it! Will one of you spit it out!" Chen was losing his cool.

"There's something in the lagoon!"

The lagoon in question was a spot where the cows went to get their water. Calves followed their mothers to the shoreline, and they gorged themselves until they were satisfied. Chen had just had the lagoon tested a month ago and the results were perfect. Now, hearing something was in it, he began to get worried.

"What do you mean there's something in the lagoon?" Chen asked.

Yuto moved aside and let Hatata say his piece despite him being more out of breath.

"It's just beneath the surface," he stammered.

"What are we talking about?"

"It. Well. It looked like a massive rock formation at first. Then it started moving."

"What? Is Godzilla in the lagoon? Quick, call Japan," Chen chuckled. "On second thought, don't."

"This is serious!" the security officer cried.

"Listen, Hatata. I know you've come all the way from Egypt on some pipedream. Here though, in the water, there's something called shadows and algae," Chen explained, patronizingly.

"I'm serious! Also, to be clear, there's water in Egypt!"

"I think it's worth investigating," Yuto stated.

Both the men's adrenaline was winding down and they wanted to take a seat. They stood standing still out of respect but were tempted.

"Why do you say that? I mean, there's nothing in the lagoon worth hunting."

"No, but the cows are."

"You think a rock monster is going to come out and attack the cows?" Chen laughed.

"There are crocodiles in the area," Yuto said.

Chen turned to Hatata. "How big would you say this apparition was?"

"It was no apparition but, if I were to base if off the parts I saw, and take a conservative guess, I'd say seventy feet."

His boss erupted in laughter. "Now I know you're putting me on! Crocs don't get that big. What's next? You're going to tell me it was a whale?"

"To be fair, boss, we never said it was a crocodile," Yuto said.

"I think you two should leave before this gets to be something I don't forget." Chen pointed a finger at them then. "Do *not* mention this to anyone."

"I'm sure we won't have to." Hatata stood up and walked out of the office.

"Can you believe him! Remind me to dock his next paycheck." Chen was seething.

Yuto nodded and got up to leave.

"Oh, and go check the lagoon for yourself. If there's something there, I'll give you both my next paycheck." He cackled like a hyena.

The associate manager ground his teeth before leaving the room. He began to rethink his position at the company. Hatata was not the only one who saw something in the lagoon.

***

Mako Zichen was like a fly hanging around dog turds. In this case, it was cows'. They reeked of pure methane and manure. He was beginning to regret taking this job. His boss implored him to do it because the last guy scatted all the way to Alaska for another story and Mako was always known for his never-say-no, can do attitude. He was getting sick of that atrocious title.

As he held his camera up to his face, he took a few snapshots of the field and cows that inhabited them. They were half-assed and would probably not leave the developing stage.

"Damn is it hot," he said to himself.

He was Taiwanese but grew up in Hong Kong. His father had relocated to a job there and he and his family packed up and moved to the area to live the glorious life of inner-city struggles.

Slapping mosquitoes that thought his neck was a free blood supplier, he began cursing to himself. "And I thought Taiwan was hot!"

The muggy environment was enough to drive any sane man at least a little mad. The bugs only added to his distain of the locale. The fresh air would have been nice had it not been coated in a blanket of thin air. It was like he was all bundled up and sitting directly under the sun during a heatwave. He could hardly even breathe sometimes.

There was one thing he had to admit. He had stopped smoking when he began his journey in journalism at the farm four months ago. It caused his lungs to burn and made it impossible to allow any airflow into his lungs.

"Damnit!" He slapped his neck again.

This time, when he pulled his hand back, he saw it was coated in blood. "How big are these fuckers?"

He decided to take a walk down to the farm itself. He was trespassing but no one checked on the cows as regularly as they should. His story was simple. He needed to find out if steroids were being used on the cows. His chief editor was friends with a rival dairy company and wanted answers as to how their cows produced such quality product. As far as Mako was concerned, it was not due to happy employees.

Maybe there was something to the steroid theory. He had seen the workers perform mundane tasks with a sense of grief and misery. There was no way they were giving it their all. There had to be more to it.

Mako stepped over the fence, making sure not to cut the fabric of his cargo pants on the barbed wire. It was a maneuver he had performed many times before. He was genuinely surprised that no one had seen him yet. Although, he had been given the layout of the area during the planning stages and he pretty much knew it by heart.

In a way, he had it made. He would sneak into the facilities at night to shower and search the kitchen for leftovers. It was not a luxurious life, but it was better than what he had back home.

Home.

A place where his father died of sheer stress, and his sister was kidnapped and never seen again. He had to keep going to provide for his mother. She was all he had left.

Lost in thought, he felt the ground become mushier as his boots began to make squelching sounds. He looked down and realized he was rather close to the pond. He had heard Chen call it a lagoon, but it was just an oversized pond as far as he was concerned.

He sat down by the water's edge and began to wash the bug blood off of his hand. He then proceeded to clean any scrapes and cuts he had endured on his daily trek.

It was when the ripples began to settle, and his eyes adjusted to the light shimmering on the surface that he saw it. It was nothing too blatant, but it was there, nevertheless. It looked like a bunch of scales that stuck out of the water like triangular teeth. It sat there for a moment before disappearing.

Gruuumph.

Mako nearly fell forward into the pond at the sound of the cow that had snuck up by his side.

"Jesus H. Christ! Don't do that!"

The cow mooed loudly. Mako never realized how loud they were. Being so close, it sounded throaty. Like an organic horn that shook the entire frame of the animal.

"Skedaddle! Get out of here!" he shouted.

It pushed past him and made its way towards the waterline.

The journalist had a feeling something big was about to happen. How big, he was not sure. Still, he backed away up the mushy hill and brought his camera to his face.

A saddened look was seen on the cow's face as it turned to him. It suddenly turned into abject terror as a gargantuan pair of jaws clamped down around its chest area.

***

Hatata saw it on the security camera. The very sight of the hideous reptile was enough to scare the wits out of him. Now he saw it munching on one of the cows. He had it on camera. No one could deny its existence now.

He reached for his radio and called in the rest of the guards. Yuto was the next call. He had to warn Chen of his farm being attacked by a menace of such magnitude that it could cause hairs to turn white at the very sight of it.

Even through the grainy footage, he could tell it was a monster. The barnacle-laden scales that were black on top, but the underneath was a tannish yellow up to the white underbelly. It looked sickly, like it had been around for centuries and seen the world for what it really was.

Two other guards, Keiko and Manchu, entered the room. Hatata jabbed a finger at the monitor and began to shout about him being right. The two men did not realize what they were looking at, at first. The footage was such bad quality that the cow appeared to be floating at first. Then they realized it had been lifted into the air in a prehistoric-looking creature's jaws.

"My god," Keiko said coldly.

"How big is that thing? What's it doing in the lagoon? How can we stop it?" Manchu was asking questions at rapid fire.

Yuto then entered the room. "Did you get it on the camera?"

"You bet your balls!" Hatata cheered.

"I think it's time to bring out the big guns," Keiko said.

"Big guns aren't going to be big enough for that abomination," Machu wondered.

"Hey," Yuto paused. "Who's that?"

There, beyond the crocodile, was a scrawly, dirty looking man who was running up the small hill.

"I dunno," Hatata stated.

"He's croc-chow as far as I am concerned," Keiko laughed. "C'mon, you guys. Let's get our guns and catch us a critter."

CHAPTER EIGHT

The luck of the draw.

Mako was taken aback by his good fortune. Not only was it not him that was eaten by that crocodile, but now he had a real story to work with. He would have a few words with that chief editor who always gave him shit stories and proceed with his plan. It was half-cooked, but he knew the score. Get a picture of the crocodile and there'd be skeptics. Get footage of the crocodile and it'd be irrefutable evidence.

He marched up the hill a bit further and turned back. The cow was kicking and mooing wildly. The crocodile took a few chomps down and blood shot out of its hide like a rocket. A crimson stream nearly splattered on Mako. Soon, the cow began to relax as if it knew there was no hope. Its legs stopped bicycling and its tongue was hanging out of its mouth. The crocodile opened its jaws in an impressive showcase of distance and bit down hard, severing the cattle's head.

"Fuck me!" Mako laughed and then covered his mouth. He did not mean to be so loud, but the sight had been so awesome, so fantastic, that the profane saying just came out.

The crocodile seemed to not take notice. It instead began to gulp down the bloodied mammal. At first, Mako thought it would not fit down its gullet. Then, it just disappeared.

Before Mako could react outwardly again, he caught himself. The ravenous reptile then began to back up, slipping further into the pond. Both were watching each other. The crocodile seemed to be staring daggers into his eyes while Mako only saw dollar signs... and a hundred-foot crocodile.

He realized his time there was up. This freak of nature was not the friendliest face and he had been there more than he was welcome.

Crack.

Mako fell back to the mushy grass as bullet after bullet whizzed past him and at the crocodile. He turned, only catching a glimpse of the group of gunmen. There only appeared to be three. They were spread a few feet apart but aiming for the same target.

Reaching for his camera, Mako began to take picture after picture. First of the gunmen, then the crocodile. He slowly backed away to get a wider view. When he was far enough back, he had his proper scaling. The guardsmen looked like tiny ants compared to the gargantuan goliath.

He kicked himself for not having his camcorder on him. It was back at his truck, just outside the compound.

There was a distinct lack of notice coming from the crocodile. It seemed as if it did not care about the puny humans' presence or their gunfire. It bounced off it like pebbles hitting its scaly skin.

The group then each grabbed a weapon from behind their back. They each had long nozzles with ends that looked like cheese graters. There were also canisters strapped to their backs that Mako had not noticed before.

"Light it up!" the man in front shouted.

As if bathed in hellfire, the crocodile took the brunt of streams of heat that were expelled from the flamethrowers.

Mako was in attendance for all of it, snapping away at the awesome sight with his camera. "That sure got its attention."

Its atttention was garnered but not the kind the gunmen wanted. When the smoke cleared, they were greeted by the sight of a mightily pissed off predator.

A sudden chill came over Mako. It was strange. The weather had been unbearable mere minutes ago. The wind had kicked up too. He almost began to wonder if he had missed some announcement about a tropical storm. Rain began to pelt the ground like a thousand stones being dropped from the sky.

All three gunmen were shielding themselves from the harsh weather. The crocodile remained motionless. It was staring at them but did not attack. After a minute, it seemed to be taking a deep breath. The exhale that came after brought with it a thunderous roar that sounded like an engine revving on a motorcycle but more guttural. What came with it was a gust of wind so powerful it sent the three gunmen flying in the air and back towards the stalls.

Mako had to hang on to a tree for support. There was no telling the magnitude of the wind shield, but it did not feel good. In fact, it felt unnatural. Like a tornado had just suddenly appeared and ripped across the pasture. He concluded that it was not Mother Nature that caused this. That would be too sporadic.

It was that damned crocodile.

Hatata was the first to get up after the wind had calmed down. To his surprise, the weather was still slamming into the rafters, causing everything to shake. He realized it calmed down within the stalls. He was afraid to even consider going back out there. Where the beast was.

The cows were mooing in hysterics. Keiko and Machu were barely aware of their surroundings, let alone what was happening. The fly-fall had been a real beating. They were both in the stalls, trying to collect themselves. One of the bigger bulls stepped back and onto Machu's foot. He cried out in agony.

That seemed to snap Keiko back into focus. His vision was a bit cloudy, so he rubbed his eyes. When it cleared, he saw colorful dots dancing around. The pigments began to fade away. Soon, he could see again. He saw Hatata getting his flamethrower prepped for another round of fire versus fury. He then turned to see the big cow stepping on Machu. He slapped it on the behind and it slowly moved away.

Ongoing rain gave way to hail as it pelted the metal sheeted roof. The sound was deafening. The three men had to cover their ears. None of them realized their torture had only just begun.

Hatata tried to fight against the wind and trudged forward towards the opening. Keiko wanted to protest but Machu grabbed his arm, squeezing it tightly. His pain was unbearable.

"No! I think my foot is broken!" he cried.

"Damnit!" Keiko spat. "Sir! We need to get Machu to a hospital, stat!"

Their boss did not seem to pay the request any mind. It was not even second thought worthy. He sneered, "I can do this."

"Since when did you become a bad ass?" Keiko said, sarcastically.

That seemed to knock Hatata's macho behavior down a peg and he turned back to his fellow guards. His friends. "It's going to destroy everything."

"… And us if we don't leave now!"

He looked down at the flamethrower and frowned. "Damn thing probably won't even work again."

Unslinging the weapon from his shoulder, he let it fall to the ground and began towards them. The look of relief on Machu's face was almost as humorous as Keiko's expression of horror. His face was contorted into an ugly look of shock and awe. Hatata turned back to see the crocodile was no longer on the ground. It was soaring through the air.

The damn thing had leapt from the lagoon to the stall in a single bound.

"What the fuck!" Hatata cried out.

A thunderous crash, louder than anything Mother Nature could produce, as the rafters and steel frames of the structure began to collapse scared Hatata. The cow enclosure would not hold. It indeed only took one impact to cave the ceiling in. A piece of rusty rooftop came down. It was a sheet of metal that cut Machu's head in two.

Keiko was not as lucky. His agony would last longer. He had managed to get up to run when the crocodile slammed down. The force of the impact, as well as the weather let in by the gaping hole in the ceiling, caused him to fly backwards and onto a thrasher. It had been tucked in there for the season. Keiko looked down at the thin spikes protruding from his chest area. He tried to speak but blood erupted from his mouth. The last thought he had was that the crimson substance was darker than he thought it would be

Hatata managed to make it a few feet before running into a calf. It toppled over and began writhing around, hooves in the air, legs kicking. It was then pelted with debris that caused its hide to be shredded down to the meat and bone underneath.

That motorcycle engine-sounding roar came again, and it all seemed to stop. The sun came out, peeking in and out of the swirling clouds as if playing peek-a-boo. Hatata did not know what was happening as he was covered in cow innards that piled nearly a foot off the ground.

He felt the ground tremor. There seemed to be a sequence of four before a gap occurred. It was four legs. The crocodile was coming. Hatata began to hyperventilate as much as possible. He thought he could smell the foul intestines through his gaping mouth. The stink was horrendous. Fresh cow guts. He knew he had to get out of there. There had to be a way. He began to shove the slippery sausage-looking links off him. Puking seemed like it would help but he knew it would only make everything smell worse.

Thud. Thud. Thud. Thud.

It was getting closer. He began to softly plead to whoever would listen. He was not a religious man but now seemed like the best time to become one. The footsteps were right next to him now. There was no escape. He had failed to save himself.

"What the hell?"

A muffled voice with a familiar tone could be heard. Hatata wasted no time.

"Help me!"

He felt a pair of hands reaching in the intestines, feeling around for a sign of life. Then, there was air. Sweet, fresh air. He got a good look at Chen who had a sour expression.

"I don't pay you to play around in cow guts!"

***

Shu and Pat arrived at the potential crime scene. They had gone over every scenario imaginable yet still came to understand why Haruto kept on about secrecy. The phone call had been distinctly vague. By the time Shu met up with Pat, they were both equally as confused as they were intrigued.

After being chaperoned by one of Haruto's deputies, they were dropped off at an inlet on the river. It was practically a cove. A very interesting discovery, not worth calling them down there though as far as they were concerned.

Haruto approached them. A bit apprehensive to even suggest there was anything wrong, he decided to take it in as logical a way as possible.

"I was alerted by Kenji Ho to investigate at least two missing kids down this river. There was a downed tree that he claims the croc had taken while snatching one of the kids off." He ushered them to follow. They did. "He showed me this area here. There were definite signs that something had made indents in the mud. Perhaps it was even a crocodile."

He showed them the indents in the mud.

"Judging by the tail length and width, the animal would have to be as large as a humpback whale," Shu explained.

"It's not possible," Pat said with authority.

"That's what I thought," Haruto began. "Kenji's over here. We both stumbled upon what I'm about to show you next. If you're worried about the size of the animal being impossible, just you wait and see."

Kenji looked up at them with a grim expression. "I promise you. This is not a hoax."

He then looked down at the ground. There was a massive imprint in the mud. Several triangular shapes rounded the top while the lower portion was somewhat oval-shaped.

"What is this?" Pat looked in disbelief.

"It's a footprint, man," Kenji stated.

The print was at least the length of an average-sized human male.

Shu seemed a bit skeptical. "Are there more?"

"Follow me," Kenji told her.

Pat followed them as well, although he was lagging. His face told it all. He had never thought it was possible for such an animal to exist on land. At least not since the time of the dinosaurs. He began to wonder if that was what it was. Some sort of creature lost to time.

He almost slammed into Shu who stopped suddenly. "What's the hold up?"

She did not respond.

After a few moments, he peered over her shoulder. There, ahead in the mud, were several more footprints. They were not that far apart which made it seem like the creature was a quadruped. They were all similarly shaped and just as big and intimidating.

"My God." Shu stood there, rigid.

"Kenji. What did this?" Pat asked.

"It's come back."

"What has?" Shu looked away from the prints.

"The crocodile that destroyed my family and home," he continued. "After the attack, I saw similar prints that were in the process of being washed away by the tide. It's not something I'd ever forget. The animal is an anomaly. No, it's more than that. It's a god incarnate."

"You can't be serious," Pat scoffed.

"It's here," Kenji said coldly "It's going to make all of Hong Kong its domain."

"Then maybe it's time we get out of its home," Shu suggested.

The three hiked back up the trail where Haruto stood with his deputy. They both looked distraught.

"We just got a call," Haruto paused. "It seems your crocodile has migrated up to the Kowloon Dairy Farm."

CHAPTER NINE

A quaint place.

Kan's seafood restaurant was always a delight. The food was scrumptious, the activities for the children, adorable. Dede sat drawing on the coloring book that was presented to her by one of the waitresses. She was having trouble coloring in the lines, a fact she brought up multiple times to Lilly who would help her every time.

Morgan was sitting across from Lilly. As he looked over the menu, he could not help but occasionally look up at her. She had put on a dark dress with red roses covering it. It covered everything except her arms and head. A typical cheongsam.

She caught fleeting glances from him and smiled each time. There was a feeling of being back in grade school and all the boys crushing over her. They played it sheepishly, much like Morgan was doing now. Except there was a difference. Morgan was older than a kid or even young adult. He was thirty-one years young.

A waitress came up and took their orders. She then returned to the kitchen.

Lilly turned to Dede. "How about you go play in the ball pit for a bit? I'll call you over when the food arrives."

"Yay!" Dede shouted.

Dashing out of there at lightning speed, she went into the playground and instantly began chatting to the other kids while having a grand old time.

Keeping her attention on Dede, Lilly was admiring her granddaughter's youth. There was admiration to be found in her spry spirit.

"It's been six years," Morgan said suddenly.

Lilly jumped in her seat. "What?"

Morgan tried to play it cool. "Every day, for six years, I've been thinking about you."

She did not respond right away.

"I remember the first time I saw you. You were just as beautiful as you are now."

Blushing fiercely, she decided to take it slowly. "Why, Mr. Stanley. I do believe you're out of line."

"Unlike Dede's drawings, I feel I've been within the lines this whole time," he chuckled, nervously.

She smiled at him. "Do you really think it's wise? You're one of my son's best friends."

"I don't mean any disrespect to him or his family. I just needed to know if you felt the same way."

Lilly wanted to shake her head, but it would be a lie. Looking was one thing, engaging in any physical activity was very much so another. Regardless, she nodded slowly. Her eyes grew watery. The truth was, she had been yearning for him for as long as he had been pondering on her.

"We can't do anything though. Can we?" Morgan wondered.

She sighed. "I wish we could. You have no idea how much I'd love that."

"Then what's stopping us? If two people like each other, they should explore it further."

"I don't think Yow would approve."

"We're not family, not even close. There'd be nothing weird about it," Morgan explained.

He could tell she was thinking about it. The way her eyes darted back and forth. It was clear there was desire that showed all over her face. Morgan almost thought she would grab him and plant a kiss on his lips right there. She still managed to play it cool. He had to give her props.

Instead, she did something unexpected. She held out her hands for Morgan to take. He reached out and placed them there. Her hands were small but her fingers, long. They were delicate and soft. She had manicured fingernails that ran an inch on the tips.

Morgan's fingers were the opposite. They were rough, callous-covered, and even somewhat hairy. He was a hard-working man. She could tell by his hands alone.

She looked at him with longing eyes. "If we do this, there's no going back."

"I would never want to."

"My room, tonight."

"Okay." He then thought about it. "What about Yow and Sang?"

"I'll give them something to sleep heavier."

"And Dede?"

"She sleeps like a rock anyway."

As if on cue, Dede approached the table. "Grandma, what's a gargantuan?"

Lilly was taken aback by the word. "What?"

"On the TV?"

Both Lilly and Morgan looked up and saw the news report. It showed the Kowloon farm. As the camera angle changed position, it turned to the stalls. They were ultimately ravaged. They could tell the camera was cutting quickly as to not show the dead cattle.

Everyone in the restaurant sat silent, their eyes glued to the television monitors. It was when the words *gargantuan creature* were spoken did everyone begin to worry.

The food arrived at the table and Dede chowed down on hashbrowns, a slice of ham, and some rice. Lilly and Morgan had lost their appetite.

***

Yow had been called half an hour ago to report to the hospital. He was barely cognizant when stepping into the shower. The cold water did not help much. He eventually got out, dried off, and looked at himself in the mirror. Despite the bags under his eyes, he looked healthy, just tired.

"Is that your professional prognosis?" Yow asked himself.

He then got dressed and made his way into the kitchen where Sang had a sandwich waiting for him.

"I'm sorry I must go. They assure me it's only going to be for a couple of hours. They've got a patient there they want a second opinion on."

"It's alright. We'll start our day when you get back." She smiled as he pecked her cheek.

She watched him go and then returned to bed.

The drive to the hospital was not too bad. The time was between the morning commute and lunch break. It took him an extra two minutes, but he arrived promptly. He then got out of his car and walked speedily inside. As far as he was concerned, he could not walk fast enough. It was ridiculous. He had put in for time off yet they treated him like he was on-call 24/7.

He entered the wing with his office in it and entered the waiting room. Both Haruto and Pat were sitting there.

"I take it that this is an official call."

"I'm going to be blunt, Mr. Chung. We have a survivor who has gone quiet."

"What do you mean?"

Pat stepped forward. "He's in shock."

"Who is he?"

"He worked at the Kowloon Dairy Farm. The boss found him in a pile of cow guts. He was nearly catatonic."

"Did he say anything?"

"Just mumbles. Then nothing more," Haruto sighed. "He's in the patient room, A4."

"I don't understand. I'm a physician. I'm not a psychiatrist. What do you need me for?"

"His injuries have been infected with fecal matter. He needs a shot and medicine," Pat stated. "We also wanted another man here in case he gets riled up."

"What kind of injuries did he sustain?"

"Cuts. Several dozens of them. They're covering his back and calves. It's almost like he was pelted with a thousand needles from behind," Pat explained.

"Sheesh." Yow held his breath briefly.

"Shall we?" Haruto asked.

The three entered the patient's room. Despite having been given a bath, the man still reeked. The earthy, muddy smell was pungent on his skin. Both Yow and Pat were okay with it, but Haruto had to cover his nose.

"What's his name?" Yow asked.

"His name is Hatata. He is one of the security guards," Haruto explained.

Unflinching at the sound of his name, Hatata remained staring transfixed on the wall ahead of him. He was facing away from the trio, his eyes boring into the tile as if he were looking past it.

"Hatata," Yow began. "I'm here to examine you and your case. Is there anything you'd like to say before I get started?"

No response.

"What attacked you?" Yow asked plainly.

There was a slight twitch in his left eye. It was as if one of the words startled him into reality.

"Was it small? Big?" The doctor's voice was calm. It seemingly soothed the big man despite his reluctance to really respond to anything. He was stoic but not unbreakable.

"Did it have scales?" Haruto asked suddenly.

Yow looked over to him. Normally he would chastise anyone for being so blunt, but it seemed to have the desired effect. Hatata's eyes grew wide with shock. The disbelief that covered his expression was immense. It was as if he was seeing something horrible that had already occurred. It was happening all over again.

"Hatata. Please try to help me understand," Yow asked.

Pat took a step forward. "I think it's in Hatata's best interest if we were to back off for now."

Either Yow did not hear him, or he did not want to hear him. He began to inch closer to the patient. He raised a hand and slowly brought it forward. "What did you see?"

There was no instant reaction when Yow's hand placed down on his shoulder. Slowly, almost methodically as if every muscle was contorting itself to shape into a face of absolute fear, his expression changed. The look of abject horror now covered him from his features to his very body temperature.

"He's cold," Yow said suddenly

"He's going into shock!" Pat shouted. "Nurse! Nurse! Get in here!"

Hatata's whole body began to tremble. The spasms were uncontrollable as he gripped the metal table beneath him. Shaking, he was seemingly writhing in pain. Then, he began to lay backwards.

"Don't let him sit back! He might swallow his tongue!" Yow shouted as he reached around Hatata to support him.

Pat aided as a nurse ran in with a sedative. The man began to calm and relax as the fluid pumped into him. In addition to this, his muttering began to sound more cohesive and audible.

"The storm came with it," he stammered.

"What storm?" Yow asked.

"The weather. It arrived shortly after it did."

"What did?" Yow was pressing harder than he meant to.

Hatata's eyes opened wide. "The crocodile."

Haruto backed away slowly as Yow and Pat continued to hold down Hatata until he settled fully. He then reached for his radio. Once out, he held down the button and spoke into it with an authoritative tone. "Deputy Ro, I need you to gather all the local fishermen with the big boats. We need to set up a bounty as well. Over."

"Roger, Sheriff. What about the mayor? Over," Deputy Ro's voice came through, childlike by comparison.

"I'm sure he can round up the cash necessary. Over."

"You got it, Sheriff. Over."

"I'll meet you at the town hall in two hours. Over and out."

Yow spun around and looked the sheriff in the eyes. "You can't be serious?"

"What choice do I have? I'm not letting my officers go out there. Only a handful fish for sport and half of *them* only do it on the weekends. We need experienced fishermen."

"I'm guessing you'll want to get in contact with Kenji Ho then?"

"I'm not opposed to it."

"That bastard should be brought up on charges for reckless boating at the very least."

"You can tell him that when you see him bring in the beast. I'd bet money on it that he'll haul that sucker in."

"Why's that?" Yow asked.

"Let's just say he's not only good at catching sharks."

***

Yow was now sitting inside the town hall with a look of annoyance. The stands he was situated in were cramped and old. Every time he moved, the wooden seats creaked, and floorboards moaned. There were other officials there with equal expressions of displeasure. Pat and Shu sat across him to his right while Haruto was to his left.

The room itself was stuffy and claustrophobia could easily set in for anyone who suffered from it. It was no longer nor wider than Yow's pool. It could hold up to ten people in the common area but Haruto had managed to squeeze thirteen, including Kenji Ho whom Yow could not tear his eyes from.

He was supposed to be at home with his family and Morgan. He was reluctant to include the American in on the whole thing. This was his vacation. Why should he have to bother with it? Still, Yow was a bit jealous that Morgan got to relax at his home with his family while he was stuck here.

Adjusting his collar, Yow decided to take a deep breath. He hoped Haruto was right and Kenji's reputation would be one the fisherman could live up to. If not, the other eleven fishermen would more than likely do the job. Yow had been informed that Kenji was blind with fear when he almost ran over his daughter. There was the idea of forgiving him but the realization that it could have been much worse kept him from doing so.

Mayor Lee stood at the podium with a few other select officials to his left. They were mostly local politicians but one of them seemed ancient. Yow assumed it was the mayor's father who had been an elected official before. There was also another man there who looked unfamiliar.

Lee raised his hands for silence, and everyone sat down.

"Now, I'm sure the rumors surrounding this meeting are wild and extravagant. I can assure you it's nothing that fantastic," Lee continued. "Several days ago, a beachgoer was killed by what we presumed was a shark. Later, some kids went missing on the Mai Po River. There was a witness who claimed it was a giant crocodile. Then, the Kowloon Dairy Farm was attacked, and two guardsmen were killed. Another was injured and claimed it to be a crocodile. This string of attacks did not go undocumented. Reports were made as were photographs taken."

The room gasped in unison.

"Pictures?" Kenji looked at him with shock and awe.

"Yes. Mind you, the photos were a bit underdeveloped but, as we will show you, it is clearly a crocodile." Lee turned to the man unfamiliar to everyone else in the room. "This is Mako. He's a reporter who was at the site of the Kowloon Dairy Farm attack."

Mako stood up and bowed.

"Lights please," Lee stated.

As requested, the room darkened. Then, a screen slid behind the podium high enough so that it would not be blocked. Then the projector turned on. Everyone's reactions were similar.

"What the hell is that?" one of the fishermen asked.

The black and white photo was covered in blemishes. There were some spots that were clear enough. Most could tell instantly that the guardsmen were firing at something. Only the front of the creature's snout and a few teeth were visible.

"It's the head of the beast," Mako stated.

"How big would you say it is?" Kenji asked.

"It was the biggest animal I had ever seen walk on dry land."

"Bigger than an elephant?" a fisherman asked.

"Almost as tall as one I'd say. The damn thing's length ran longer than any constrictor ever recorded."

"Are we talking twenty feet?"

"Maybe... When it was a newborn," Mako chuckled.

Kenji's eyes did not leave the picture. He seemed lost in it. He was still cognizant enough to listen and ask questions though. "Do you have any more photos like this one?"

"None as good. I guess I did not realize how much the weather had affected my camera."

"Did the weather..." Kenji gulped. "Did it arrive when the crocodile attacked?"

Mako appeared as if he did not want to answer. He could tell when people were on the verge of losing it. Kenji was hanging over that ledge. Still, he knew he could not be dishonest to the man. "It was quite the coincidence, I must say."

The fisherman's face turned ghostly pale. "It's the same one."

"Listen, Kenji. We all know what happened on Habito Island," Lee stated.

Kenji shook his head in disbelief. Shu watched him. Her sympathy covered her face in grief. She had never seen a man so lost and afraid. This hardened hunter was now vulnerable, nearly cowering in his boots.

"It must be stopped," he said suddenly. "The damage it will cause, families, homes, will be haunting the generations to come."

"That is what I am proposing. I want you fishermen to hunt down and kill this crocodile. No matter what it takes." Lee looked to Kenji. "I will personally supply you with a ship worthy of hunting it. It'll be a lot better than that dinky speedboat you drive around."

All Kenji could do was nod in thanks.

"What's the reward?" a few of the fishermen asked simultaneously.

"180,000 Yuan."

"Seems mighty steep for going after a predator such as this."

Kenji turned to the fisherman and spat at him. "It should be for free. This thing will take everything you have. You need to realize what you're up against."

The fisherman wiped the saliva from his nose and stared daggers into Kenji's eyes. "I'm not going to risk my life for free!"

"200,000 Yuan is my final offer," Lee announced.

All the fishermen nodded in agreement except Kenji.

"Have fun with your lives. What's left of them." He then stormed towards the doors.

"Where are you going?" Lee shouted.

Kenji turned and looked at the mayor. "If all else fails, you know where to find me."

He then pushed through and made his way down the street and towards his fishing shack.

CHAPTER TEN

Imprisoned.

Crashing waves caused Kenji to stir in his restless sleep. The demon of the past infiltrated his subconscious. Mountains of seawater with traces of red cascaded over him in a violent thrashing affair. The smell of ocean permeated the air as the saltwater stung his eyes and burned his nose.

Gouts of gore came after. Body parts, limbs for as far as the eye could see. Trailing sinew and tattered flesh in their wake, they seemed to be ushered by the waves towards him as he sat on the beach.

In his arms he cradled a bundle of cloth. The contents of it were clear. Hai was alive and well and he had to protect him.

Then the roaring came.

The crocodile glided across the surface. Ripples of water brushed against its scales. Its tail swayed back and forth, causing froth to appear. The sloshy foamy liquid only intensified as it quickened its pace. The great predator was mere feet from the beach now.

Kenji could not figure out how to stand. His legs felt like Jell-O. The wobbly dance he performed was almost comical if not for the dire situation he was in. Suddenly, he collapsed under his own weight and crushed the bundle beneath him.

He heard a woman's scream as he tried to lift himself off the ground.

"You killed him!"

Dala's voice was shrill as her eyes began to form irreversible tears. The pain etched on her face haunted him where he stood.

"You murderer!"

Kenji managed to pull the bundle from under him and looked at it. Hai's face was covered in scratches and bruises. It looked as though he had been beaten by shrapnel and flakes of wood and other debris. It was not his doing that killed this child.

"It wasn't me! I know it wasn't me!"

"Murderer!" Dala screamed.

"You're wrong!"

"The crocodile! It'll take everything you care about!" Dala was chanting now.

"It already has."

"Then kill yourself!"

He froze. "You're not Dala!"

"No, I'm not." The imposter began to laugh.

He spun around and ran up to her. She looked familiar but it was clearly not Dala.

"Give them back! I will not die!"

"They're already gone," her voice croaked.

"No! They can't be!"

"Yes. They left this morning," the intruder's voice suddenly changed.

Kenji blinked a few times, and his vision began to clear. Shu was standing before him.

"Are you alright now?" she asked. Her face was full of fear and confusion.

"I'm... I'm sorry. Uhm. What time is it?" He looked around for a clock but then realized he did not have one.

"It's almost seven in the morning."

Kenji looked around and saw that light was pouring in from the ceiling.

"They left an hour ago."

"Who?"

"The fishermen," Shu continued. "A couple of locals saw the croc making its way out to sea from the Kowloon Dairy Farm. Four boats went out to stop it from hurting anyone else."

He shook his head. "It won't be enough."

***

Jaw-Long sat in the wheelhouse of the Dragon Hide. His teeth were constantly clenching at the thought of what they would be facing. He did not need any fancy equipment or high-tech gear to stop the crocodile, but he feared the others might.

Four fishing boats, real tanks of the sea, were pushing through the current as they cleared the second checkpoint. Soon, they were out in open water.

To the Dragon Hide's right was the Pleasure Fisher. Captain Zimo and his first mate Rui were two of the most pleasant fishermen in the game. That good attitude did not reflect their bank accounts. They were a crew of two and barely making ends meet. They had to let go of their third sailor on account of profit margins and him being too green. Still, they functioned enough without him.

There were two boats to Jaw-Long's left. The furthest was the Crawler. He did not know much about them other than their inexperience. Their boat was fresh off the lot and so were they. They were a crew of four greenhorns. The closest to the Dragon Hide's left was the Vendetta. Jaw-Long's brother, Zichen, captained it along with the only other member of the crew, Xiaobo who was the shortest man any of them had ever seen. He stood three-foot-eight and had the attitude of a chihuahua.

Zichen had had a chip on his shoulder ever since he and Jaw-Long's father passed. He had left the latter his boat and a future while Zichen received a small shack on the water in desperate need of maintenance. There was hostility between them now. Calling the boat Vendetta made Zichen's intentions clear.

At least he was the only one who could afford a sonar monitor.

"Any sign of 'em?" Xiaobo called out to his captain.

"Not a peep on here or out there," Zichen nodded over towards the sea.

"Maybe it won't show?"

"What's the matter? Ya scared?"

"I'm not afraid of no reptile!" Xiaobo laughed. Deep down, he was fuming with his severe case of anger issues.

"You got visual?" Jaw-Long's voice came over the radio.

Zichen reached up and grabbed the radio. He then clicked the button to talk into it but stalled momentarily. He then told him what he was thinking. "Even if I did, I wouldn't tell you."

"Aw. That's real brotherly of you, Zichen," Jaw-Long stated. *"I guess I'll have to do likewise."*

There was a click as Jaw-Long hung up. Zichen began to grind his teeth.

"That bastard doesn't know squat," Xiaobo told him.

"I know that!" his captain shouted and then turned to look at him. "He always has a trick up his sleeve though."

Aboard the Dragon Hide, Jaw-Long could not help but chuckle. "Lazy mooch doesn't know his asshole from his elbow."

His two crewmembers, Bolin and Ming, came up behind him.

"Is the winch ready?" he asked them.

"Yes," Bolin stated. "So is the bait."

"Excellent. Ming, are the special weapons prepared?"

Ming nodded. "Just be careful. Don't want to let them go when you're not ready."

"I'm aware," Jaw-Long smiled. "I have a feeling Zichen's fancy equipment won't be of much use to him when we reel in pieces of this crocodile!"

Bolin and Ming cheered in unison.

Jaw-Long then saw the Crawler slow its pace. He wanted to call them in but figured better. They were probably assuming they saw something. "Damn greenhorns."

The Pleasure Fisher was closest to the Crawler and could hear shouting and complaining. Zimo pulled up alongside them.

"What's the trouble, guys? See some seaweed?"

"Worse!" one of them whined. "We're out of fuel."

"What are you talking about?" Zimo suppressed a laugh.

"I filled it this morning, I swear!" another one of the four-man crew shouted.

They began to erupt into a fit of pointing fingers. Zimo pushed on the throttle and drove the Pleasure Fisher away as fast as he could.

"I don't know why Mayor Lee even hired them?" Rui wondered.

"I guess someone's got to be used as bait," Zimo chuckled.

"That's dark." Rui could not help but smirk.

***

"You can't blame yourself," Shu told Kenji who was still sitting on his cot.

Shu had found a bucket and turned it upside down to sit on. As she situated herself atop the uncomfortable makeshift chair, she watched him intently. He was bathed in sweat and seemed to be reminiscing about a thousand ghosts of people he could not save. The cultivating spirits who tormented and taunted him every night. They swarmed him with visions of some horrible past.

Kenji spoke slowly. "I don't. They do."

"Who?"

"The apparitions in my nightmares."

"Who were they?" she asked.

He did not reply.

"You seem like an intelligent man," she smiled. "Why don't you tell them to just go away?"

"Dala beckons to me every night," Kenji began. "Hai is wailing in her arms like a child lost to his future. There was nothing for him to look forward to. The same as my brother, my parents, my grandmother and all the other villagers of Habito Island. They were all swept away."

"I know. By the freak hurricane."

"It was no hurricane!" he shouted. "At least, not of Mother Nature's doing."

There was a brief reprieve of silence between them. Kenji did not want to continue, and Shu was trying to figure out how to approach her next question. He did not give her the chance as he stood up and made his way over to the center of the room.

"Why do you want a profession looking over crime scenes, Shu?"

"I guess because I want to find the truth," she replied.

"I see." Kenji nodded. "Is there any chance of my story becoming the truth? At least in your mind?"

"I believe you about a massive crocodile more than ever before. I am having a hard time thinking it can control weather."

"It is no mere reptile! It is a God!" Kenji cried out. "A god created by an old sea witch back in the 1700s!"

"What are you talking about?" Shu was worried about the man's sanity and temper.

"The legend of the Great Crocodile! It was once a demon harbored by the gods to unleash upon a pestilence ridden world when the day arrived. However, a witch who lived by the sea found a spell to conjure the creature up and use it for her own gain. She was stopped when the spell was almost completed. The crocodile has been in sort of a limbo between heaven and hell. Something must have unleashed it upon us now."

"That's crazy!"

"Times are changing, Shu!" Kenji continued. "Everything old is out, including religion. Who's to say the gods did not decide to finally unleash the beast into the modern day. It would give people enough fear to turn back to them."

"I can't believe that! It's too fantastical!"

"The power of this beast is awesome. Nothing can stop it. Those fishermen   won't   stand   a   chance."
"They already left!" Shu was panicking now.

"Then I pray they're religious." Kenji sighed and looked up through the crack in the ceiling. The sun was peeking down on him.

CHAPTER ELEVEN

A bad attitude.

The side of Mother Nature Zichen hated the most was the wind. It was always too aggressive and made chills run down his spine. There was nothing to gain from it besides pushing weather in different directions. As far as Zichen was concerned, it could go away.

Xiaobo was the opposite. He did not care if it were summer or winter, the wind had no effect on his attitude. It was the rain that did that. Bad weather meant no fishing. No fishing meant no paycheck or food on the table. He did not mind fishing in the rain. In fact, he implored Zichen to go out in it several times, but he was seemingly afraid to get wet. Xiaobo never understood him in that way. His captain was as easy to read as a children's book. The weather seemed to bring out the worst in him though.

Out of nowhere, a huge gust swept past the Vendetta, causing her to lean towards the portside.

"Damnit!" Zichen shouted.

"Wind's pickin' up," Xiaobo stated.

"No shit."

"I thought the skies were supposed to be clear today?" Jaw-Long's voice came over the radio.

"Likewise," Zichen said to himself.

The wind whirled around, causing updrafts that knocked over some buckets.

"Son of a bitch!" Zichen snapped.

"I got it, I got it." Xiaobo picked up the bucket and then sat on it.

Howling harsh air ripped through the cabin. It caused papers and even an empty metal full of coffee to tip over.

"Stop!" Zichen screamed.

"I don't think that'll work," Xiaobo chuckled.

His humor was short lived as he felt the first of the raindrops. "Oh no," he snarled.

Bloop.

Despite the increasingly bad weather, Zichen still heard the sonar pick up a massive object. His attention snapped towards it. There was nothing there. No crocodile-shaped masses. There were some small fish, maybe a tuna, and a coral reef on the ocean floor.

"Thing's bugging out again." Zichen was tempted to slam a clenched fist atop it but thought better.

"Time for a new sonar, huh?" Xiaobo was now drenched and making his way into the cabin.

"Want to cough up the money for one?" Zichen laughed and then slapped the side of it as lightly as his anger would allow.

Bloop.

Everything was the same.

He brought the boat to a slow. Looking around, he saw the Crawler and Pleasure Fisher were close together but far enough apart to do their own respective hunt. Dragon Hide was way ahead of them. There was nothing on the surface. No large scaly mass pressing against the frothy waves or bright yellow eyes watching them intently.

The sonar then made a scratching sound. Zichen looked and saw the image for a split second before it went black. The fish were still there. The coral reef was gone. It was not possible. Their boat was stopped.

"Oh shit!" Zichen cursed softly. "Xiaobo! Get up here! It's here!"

Reaching quickly, he reached for the radio. The button was down, and he was about to speak into it when he heard the first explosion. The sound of the wooden hull of the Crawler breaking entered his ears. Four fishermen's cries were drowned out by the sound of the splashing water and cracking of the boat's frame.

Xiaobo ran out of the cabin. His black hair was whipping all around, but he still saw it. The boat was in two halves and sinking fast. The four crewmembers were in the water splashing around.

"They're not going to make it." Xiaobo stood there, shocked.

Zichen paid him no mind as he started the engine. It roared to life as did the Pleasure Fisher's which was making a b-line for the crew.

"Get the guns ready!" Zichen hollered over the wind.

His crewman thankfully snapped out of it. He then darted towards a box under the seats and fished out two rifles.

"Did you see that thing?" Rui shouted.

"Yes," Zimo said.

"We can't possibly take it on!" Rui laughed exasperatedly.

"Get the rifle, Rui," Zimo ordered.

"Captain. We can't…"

Zimo snapped in his direction. "The Pleasure Fisher never abandons a fight. Or any other fishermen in distress."

Rui looked at him, ashamed of himself and afraid.

"Now get the god damn rifle!"

It did not take long for the Fisher Pleasure to approach the downed vessel and her crew. One of the four was already missing and the water was red.

"Get them out of there!" Zimo told Rui who was busy aiming his rifle at the water.

"Do you want me to shoot or save?""Put the gun down. Get them out. Then start shooting!"

Rui did as he was told and bent over to put the rifle down. By the time he looked back over the side, the three fishermen were gathered near the starboard side of the hull.

"Get them out of there!"

The rush of water that sprayed Rui felt like a million pounds. It was a wall of sea froth, blood, and scales. An aquatic nightmare. Rui fell backwards onto the deck, landing directly on his tailbone. He hollered in pain. By the time he could see three feet in front of him again, he was silent.

A chunk of the Pleasure Fisher's starboard siding had been ripped off. Rui quickly made his way to peer over the side. The remaining three fishermen of the Crawler were gone.

"It ate them! It ate them all at once!" Rui's teeth chattered.

"Get the rifle!" Zimo ordered again.

"No! You get us out of here!"

Zimo stepped away from the wheel and climbed down the ladder. "We need to kill that crocodile and avenge the crew!"

The Vendetta pulled up next to them.

"What happened? Where are they?" Zichen asked.

"They're all gone," Rui cried.

Without missing a single beat, Zichen looked over to Xiaobo. "Get the bastard."

His crewman aimed his rifle at the water as he drove the boat around the kill spot. Zimo followed suit. The water was still frothing in that area.

"Open fire!" Zichen shouted.

Both Xiaobo and Rui followed orders just as the crocodile's head appeared in the surf. They shot round after round into it.

"There's something in its mouth!" Rui noticed.

As if it knew it was caught red handed, it opened its mouth wide. It was almost in a yawning fashion. Inside, were the pulverized, mangled corpses of the Crawler's crew.

The jaws then snapped shut with a resounding slapping sound. Xiaobo screamed in defiance and aimed at the crocodile again. Each bullet found its mark but bounced off the reptile's scaly hide like it were a Tic Tac.

"Get us out of here!" Rui screamed in horror.

Zichen started the Vendetta's engine and began to drive off. The Pleasure Fisher remained stationary.

"What are you doing? Go!" Rui was tearing up now.

"I'm trying!"

The sound of the engine trying to start filled Rui's ears.

"You're going to flood it!"

Zimo ignored him and continued to try and start the boat. The wind intensified and Rui turned back to see the crocodile was a mere two feet from the boat's stern. His scream was so ear piercing that it forced Zimo to turn around.

Unmoving, the crocodile watched them with angry eyes. It looked at them as if it were furious they dared to even attempt to hurt it. Water began to slush and froth around it as a roaring sound could be heard off in the distance.

"What's it doing?" Xiaobo called up to Zichen.

Zichen peered over his shoulder. "I don't want to find out."

"Zichen, brother, are you there?" Jaw-Long's voice came over the radio again.

He did not answer.

"Zichen! Get out of there! Fast!"

He reached for the radio and spoke into it. "What do you think I'm trying to do?"

"Faster! There's something coming up from behind it!"

"What?"

"It looks like a massive wave!"

Despite being well over half a mile away from the Pleasure Fisher, neither Zichen nor Xiaobo could see what he was talking about.

"I don't see anything!" Zichen said.

"You don't understand. The water is coming from directly behind the crocodile!"

"That's not possible."

"You're telling me! Get out of there! Now!"

Zichen pushed the throttle up to its limit. The rain was now pelting hard. It sounded like rocks hitting the deck. Xiaobo placed his hands on the transom and watched as the water rushed over the crocodile and slammed directly onto the Pleasure Fisher.

"Fuck me!"

The water was still coming. It looked like a snake slithering across the surface. Its speed was faster than any boat could go.

"No. No. No!" Xiaobo backed away.

It rose up, towering over the boat.

"Oh my god!" Xiaobo cried out.

Then, as soon as it arrived, it slipped back beneath. Behind it, was the crocodile. It opened it jaws which came crashing down onto the Vendetta.

"No!" Jaw-Long cried.

"Did that thing just teleport?" Bolin wondered.

"We have to go help!" The captain ignored him and began to make a wide turn.

"Don't!" Ming pleaded. "We can't kill that thing!"

"Get the grenades ready!" Jaw-Long ordered. "Nothing like a ball of shrapnel to start your morning!"

As he drove closer towards the site of the attack, the crocodile slowly slipped under the surface. It looked so otherworldly. The whole frame of the creature was bulky beyond just the scales. Its nose had two humps that sprouted water out of its sinus cavity, the teeth lined outside the upper jaw, giving it a devious grin the whole time. The eyes were what scared Jaw-Long the most. They were a fiery orange yellow. He did not want to imagine what they looked like at night.

Once the crocodile was completely submerged, Zichen and Xiaobo breached the surface. It was as if some force had held them down there until the beast returned to its watery domain. The two fishermen swam over to the upturned Vendetta and climbed. They were having trouble on the slippery hull, but Xiaobo managed to get up first. He had something in his hand.

"Come back!" Jaw-Long could hear Xiaobo scream as the Dragon Hide drew nearer.

He noticed what he had.

"Damnit, Xiaobo! Don't do anything crazy. You're not going to kill it with a dinky knife."

The fisherman did not seem to hear him. Zichen was finally atop the hull next to him when the crocodile could be seen again. The full length of its snout was sticking out of the water. Its mouth was seemingly inviting Xiaobo in. It roared.

It dawned on Jaw-Long that it was the first time the crocodile had made any sound. So haphazardly had it destroyed the other boats that there was no real effort or desire involved. It was clear now though that it wanted one thing. Xiaobo.

The man in question screamed back at the crocodile in defiance and then took a few steps back. Zichen looked up to see his small friend preparing to lunge at it and wanted to stop him. He reached up but had to place his hand back down to steady himself on the slippery hull.

Xiaobo then ran towards the water. The knife was raised above his head and his face was frozen in a permanent rage of defiance. The crocodile accounted for his pace and trajectory and opened its mouth wide.

Zichen did not even see Xiaobo disappear down the gullet. He was there one minute and then disappeared into the black void the next.

"No!" He loosened his grip and slid off the Vendetta's hull.

"Over here!" It was Bolin.

He looked over and saw the crewmember was reaching for him while Ming provided cover. Jaw-Long stared at his brother as if telling him to get a move on.

The crocodile dove again and, this time, it did not reemerge. Zichen began to kick wildly with his feet. He brought his arms over his head in a swimming motion, but he knew he would not be fast enough. Bolin called to him.

Jaw-Long wanted to help but he knew that, once Zichen was aboard, they would need to peel out of there.

Zichen felt the slippery grasp of Bolin's sweaty forearm as he began to pull him out of the water.

Suddenly, Ming opened fire. The crocodile was further out than expected. It was as if it were giving them time to attempt to save him. Its body swayed back and forth causing small wavelets to roll around it. Ming continued to shoot but it did nothing.

"Pull him up!" Jaw-Long cried out.

Ming abandoned the firearm and reached down to help Bolin pull Zichen into the boat. They yanked and pulled but the man's waterlogged clothes added at least ten more pounds on him. The crocodile was close now. They could smell its hideous breath. Any second and it could pick up speed and slam into the Dragon Hide and take Zichen, effectively crippling the last boat to get out of there.

Bolin got ahold of Zichen's belt buckle and managed to lift him fast. Ming soon did the same. They pulled until he was over the transom and on the deck. Jaw-Long wasted no time and began to speed out of there.

The crocodile rammed into the vessel, nearly capsizing it with one blow. The metal hull was too strong and withstood the blunt force, for now. Jaw-Long managed to righten the vessel and continue the journey towards shore. The coastline was visible, but all the houses and hotels looked like small shacks along the beach. He pushed the Dragon Hide as fast as she could go but, even still, the reptile was gaining on them.

Bolin produced a grenade and pulled the pin; he then tossed it at the beast. It went off with no effect. Ming did the same with similar results.

"I swear I hit right next to its ugly eye!" Ming cried.

"Throw it in its mouth or in front of its face. Anything to slow it down!" Jaw-Long cried.

Seemingly gaining speed as if it were granted it by a supernatural force, the crocodile burst towards them.

Jaw-Long swerved the boat to the right and the crocodile brushed past them on their left.

"That was too close!" Zichen cried out.

"Then do something so it doesn't happen again!" Jaw-Long scolded his brother.

Zichen wanted to argue but decided against it. He looked around for a weapon, but his eyes kept falling onto the box of grenades. "Let me see one of those!"

He reached into the box just as a shadow cast over him. The boat was still driving, and the sky was cloudless. He looked up and saw that its tail was hovering in the air above them. It came down with tremendous force. The deck splintered a bit as the consol and upper deck were smashed to pieces. Jaw-Long had fallen backwards into Zichen's arms.

Bolin and Ming watched as the crocodile slowly swam away, its tail seemingly waving them goodbye as it slithered across the deck and then fell into the sea.

"What do we do now?" Zichen screamed as he pushed Jaw-Long off of him.

The captain got up and looked down at his brother. "We fight."

"We die, you mean?" Zichen laughed.

"If we can take the crocodile out with grenades, then we'll win and get that reward money," Jaw-Long explained.

"You're still worried about the money?" You're insane!" Zichen was bellowing now.

"It's coming back!" Ming cried as everyone turned to follow his pointing finger.

Indeed, the beast was there but it was not moving.

"I think it's waiting for us to make our move," Bolin said.

Jaw-Long looked around for the rifle and found it sticking out from the hole in the cracked deck. He scooped it up and aimed.

"Don't!" Zichen pleaded.

It was too late.

There was a shot taken but it was unclear if it was a direct hit. The crocodile took it as a sign to attack and began charging for the Dragon Hide.

"This is it!" Jaw-Long scowled.

Bolin and Ming looked at each other then to Jaw-Long. "It was a pleasure, Captain."

Zichen did not know where to go. He felt as trapped as a fish in a glass bowl.

Then it came. The crocodile impacted with the Dragon Hide at full speed. Bolin was knocked into the water while Ming fell backwards and smashed his head on the bait box. Blood oozed out from the gaping wound in his cranium. Zichen and Jaw-Long grabbed for anything to hold themselves aboard.

Maneuvering to the bow with all the intensity of a hound cornering a coon, the crocodile managed to scoop up Ming's corpse and swallow it. The bow then lifted off the water. Zichen looked to Jaw-Long. He then turned to the grenade in his hand.

"It's breakfast time." Jaw-Long laughed as Zichen pulled the pin.

Releasing the boat from under it, the crocodile backed off.

Bolin looked up and realized where he was. The Dragon Hide came down atop him, caving his skull into his shoulders.

Boom.

CHAPTER TWELVE

It was done.

An explosion was heard all the way on shore. The costal bay area was alive with commotion as onlookers observed the scene before them. Some of them had kept tabs on the boats all morning, wondering about the suspicious activity. Most were oblivious to the goings on in the sea and behind closed doors. Some people stared dumbfounded; most were startled.

Kenji Ho was looking out the window, directly where it happened when the grenade went off. He had just glanced in that direction and did not see the crocodile. He did see the boat ripped apart, but he assumed it was by the explosion.

Shu nearly fell off the bucket she was sitting on at the sound of the Dragon Hide being blown to smithereens. She managed to catch herself and turned to Kenji who looked equally shocked.

"I can't believe it!" Kenji felt a chill run down his spine. "The boats. They're all gone."

"What?" Shu got up and ran to see if what he was saying was true.

All four fishing boats were gone. Only pieces remained. From what they could see, there were no survivors.

"Did they kill it?" Shu asked.

"You can't kill a god." Kenji stepped closer to the window. He stretched himself as far out as he could see. There was a red tint in the water. He could not believe it. They had done it. He let out a scream of defiance that chilled Shu to her very core.

It was finally over. The pent-up rage and self-blame. The countless nights deprived of sleep and haunted by nightmares, visions of the past. He relaxed as he realized he could finally find peace again.

***

Questions were left unanswered. Citizens asked why there was an explosion, yet they were met with the same answer every time. It was a fishing accident involving a hand grenade.

The families of the fishermen were understandably distraught, and Mayor Lee offered them compensation and support for their inevitable tragic mental journey. The press ate it up while most of the families declined the offer. They were too humble to take it.

Mako sat back on his swivel chair in the office. He was content with his secret despite his boss wanting him to exploit it to the world. *In due time,* he had told him. As he leaned forward on his desk, he shoveled a scoop of noodles into his mouth with chopsticks.

Chief Editor Maru walked over to him and smiled. "Hey there, Mako. We need to have a talk."

"Another one?"

"Yes. I know and I respect you wanting the story to be released later but I do have an alternative for the time being."

He placed his chopsticks down. "I'm listening."

"Release the pictures. We'll put it out there in the skeptic column."

"I didn't know we had a skeptic column," Mako chuckled.

"We do if you give me those pictures to work with," Maru smiled insidiously.

"You've seen them. They're no good."

"Well, the public needs to know something. There's been damage to the Kowloon Dairy Farm and now these fishermen have died. They were not *that* far apart."

"Stranger things have happened."

"True. But usually there isn't evidence to suggest otherwise."

Mako looked down at his drawer then reached forward to pull the prints out. "If I do this, I want full rights to the images."

"I'll have it to you in writing this afternoon."

"This morning," he demanded. "I know how fast the editors work. They'll have this on the market before lunchtime."

Maru sighed. "I'll have it to you in twenty minutes."

"Sounds good." He relinquished the pictures to him. "Oh, and one more thing."

"What's that?" Maru asked while looking over them.

"Don't say anything about a crocodile."

"You afraid to cause a panic, an uproar?"

"Something like that." Mako returned to his noodles.

***

Lilly had waited for him all night. The urgency of it all made her impatient as she watched the clock near the door tick away. Soon, she could wait no more and settled in for the night where she tossed and turned in her bed.

It was a waste of the sleeping pills she had slipped into Yow's drink. They worked, for Sang said she had had a hard time waking him up the next morning. She was not sure she could get away with it again.

Still, she kept her faith in Morgan. Praying for him to enter her room with the urge to take her in his arms where they would spend the night. It made her feel warm inside. The notion of it potentially happening drew her to giving her son a second pill. This time, she gave Sang one too.

Now she lay on the bed and wondered what it would be like. He was right next door to her and the act of it all seemed so forbidden. The fear of being caught slipped away as soon as she heard the door creak open.

She was facing the window and wearing a burgundy Cheongsam dress.

"Hello," he said in a somewhat seductive tone.

"What took you so long?" she asked innocently.

"I think you gave the pill to the wrong person."

Lilly thought back and realized it was entirely possible. Yow was already tired when he got home from the extra shifts he had picked up at the hospital. It stood without reason that he would be harder to waken.

She gasped. "I'm so sorry."

Turning to face him, she was taken aback. He was wearing the black speedo he wore at the beach. His throbbing erection was clearly visible.

"What can I do to help you forgive me?"

He carefully shut the door behind him. As he strode across the room, he admired her. Her dress fit tightly around her figure but there were slits on the sides of her hip. A gap held together by a tight knot allowed for a glimpse of her chest to be shown. His manhood seemed to grow even further when he saw the outline of her buxom chest being hugged by satin material.

On the dress were golden dragons. They were not too distracting and blended in with the mastery of the piece all together.

"I forgive you just by looking at you."

Out of nowhere, she let out an uncontrolled whimper. It almost sounded like a moan coming from her sweet, raspy voice.

Soon, he stood before her. He held out his hands and she took them. She guided him to sit next to her which he did without hesitation. He then reached up and cupped a hand along her cheek. She rubbed against it.

"Six years," he whispered to her softly.

"It's been long enough." She leaned forward and planted a kiss on his lips.

Soon, their tongues danced around in each other's mouths. Morgan placed his other hand on her face and held her closer. They lay back on the bed while kissing, inseparable. She placed a hand on his chest and felt down towards his groin. Her hand slipped inside his speedo, and she began to rub his shaft carefully.

It was his turn to moan now as their lips parted.

Morgan then flipped the flap of her dress up and gazed down at her hairy crotch. He inched closer and she guided him inside her. She groaned loudly as he pushed further in. He then brought it back and forth. She could not stop making noise, so he muffled the lustful sounds by kissing her again.

Soon, he was on top of her and thrusting madly. Lilly covered her mouth but was finding it hard to breathe. Then he pulled a maneuver she did not expect. He ejaculated inside her.

She stopped and looked at him, visibly tense.

"I'm sorry."

"I'm not on the pill."

He could only repeat himself. "I should have pulled out. I should have paced myself. I'm sorry."

Reaching around his shoulder, she placed a delicate hand on his chest and rubbed. "It's okay. I'll deal with whatever comes of it."

"Please don't have an abortion. I want a piece of me to always be with you."

"A memory would have been fine."

"I don't want to just be a memory. I want to be with you!" Morgan stated.

"Shhh." She paused. "I don't think Yow would approve."

"We're all adults who make our own decisions."

She nodded. "I think you should go to your own room. I need time to think."

"Okay." He leaned forward and kissed her on the cheek. Soon, he was gone and Lilly sat there brooding in her own thoughts.

Why did he do it? she wondered. *There had to have been, an ulterior motive. There was no amount of lust in the world to make a man want to have a child with a woman he barely knew.*

She then thought about the whole thing. Initially, she wondered if the one-night stand would end up being just a fluke. He seemed serious in the passionate throes he performed. The way he watched her was filled with intentions. She knew he loved her on the outside. He did not seem to let it sink in that she was a mother to an adult not much younger than himself.

Another part of her felt it was cute in a helpless romantic sort of way. It was perfectly healthy to be attracted to older women as well. *Maybe he's insecure?* She already had one son; she did not need to take care of another grown man.

Then, she thought about what he did to her. She knew she was not young but that did not mean she could not get pregnant. The turmoil in her mind swirled around like a whirlpool.

She lay on her back and hoped she would drift off into sleep, but she found herself restless and somewhat upset with herself. She could not blame Morgan, could she? It was desire that brought those actions about. She was not sure if it was the desire to be with her or to have a family.

Lilly then thought about her own feelings towards the man. She had thought about him sometimes during those years, but he seemed to relish in the memories of her. She wanted him but needed to know more about him in order to commit.

Good going, Lilly. You should have done that before you slept with him, she inwardly scolded herself.

That was it though. She could not help herself either. She gave her son and daughter-in-law sleeping pills. She knew what she wanted and what she was getting into.

She closed her eyes and, slowly but surely, drifted off to sleep.

***

"These men had a lot of guts!" the dredger, Tacu, shouted above the sound of the roaring waves. "Externally and internally."

"That's not funny at all!" Haruto replied over the radio.

"Yeah, well you aren't paying me and my team for our sense of humor, Sheriff," Tacu laughed.

"I shouldn't have had to pay you at all."

"That's politics for you," Tacu said.

After the explosion, the police department received countless death threats and other harassments. Most from grieving families, others from the government. They felt Haruto went behind their backs and offered a generous reward for the destruction of the crocodile. Now they made him pay for a cleanup crew.

Haruto was not appreciative of this but held his tongue. There was always light at the end of the tunnel. It still stung though.

"Just get the job done."

"Technically we already did. You wanted a second comb over."

"That's right. There were no signs of the crocodile. I need a corpse. Or, at the very least, pieces of a corpse."

"Hey. It's your dime," Tacu chuckled.

"Don't remind me." Tacu heard Haruto hang up the radio with a resounding click.

"I guess we keep dredging?" Masa asked.

Tacu looked at his small crew which included Masa and another fellow he never got a chance to meet formally. He had been assigned to him last minute because they were short staffed.

"You're correct. Although, I'm not going into overtime for this. The company would not have it."

"I thought the sheriff was paying for everything?"

"The company doesn't know that, and I intend to keep it that way. As far as I'm concerned, the sheriff is paying our overtime while we still stay within hours."

Masa and the other man nodded.

"Let's get this thing hauled up so we can go ashore and spend the money," Tacu laughed.

The three drove around finding body parts and intestines galore. None were big enough to belong to a crocodile.

Masa was visibly growing bored. Tacu took note of it to scold him later. Dredging was a serious business and required the team to be alert. He did have to hand it to the new guy. He kept a razor-sharp focus on the sea and all the instruments on the boat.

"What's your name?" he called to him.

The man grunted. "Busy."

"Busy? That's an odd name."

"We need to find out if the crocodile has been destroyed."

"Why is it so important to you?" Masa chuckled.

"Because it killed my cousin, Xiaobo."

"Was he part of the fishing expedition?"

The man nodded. "He suffered from dwarfism but was as bitter as an old sailor."

"Well, we need to keep personal vendettas aside. Keep in mind, we are just a clean up crew," Tacu explained.

He grunted again.

His mind was in focus, yet he still missed the large chunk of flesh that bumped alongside the hull. Masa ran over with a gaff and hooked it.

"What you got there?" Tacu asked.

Masa hefted it with the extent of his strength, the man then aided him by grabbing part of the pull. Together, they hauled it aboard.

It was enormous. It was two feet wide and three feet long. It had black scales laden along the top while beneath was soft pink flesh.

"It's a chunk from the crocodile!" Masa cheered. "The damn thing's been blown to smithereens."

The other man examined it closer. There were marks that landed along the scales. It was as if they had been torn by shrapnel. *It was destroyed by the grenade, they were successful.*

"Looks like we're bringing back good news, boys!" Tacu smiled.

CHAPTER THIRTEEN

A new dawn.

Spreading across the sky with all the glory of a god, touching clouds that were shaped like angel wings, the sun brought about change. Change to the day that welcomed all forms of life. From the tiny shrew to the man that walked out of his room and towards the kitchen.

Morgan Stanley tried to find embrace in the sun's glow but found only annoyance as it made him squint his eyes. He looked out into the yard. There was a pool with lounge chairs surrounding it and umbrellas abound. He imagined Lilly Chung sunbathing and he felt a stirring in his night robe.

He poured himself a glass of milk to start the day. It was cold and refreshing as it went down his throat. He then washed the dish and turned to see a figure sitting on the couch in the den. Her dark hair had a nice wave to it and she was wearing a light pink, satin robe that hugged her back nicely.

"You're up early," he said.

She jumped slightly but maintained composure.

"Yes. I couldn't sleep."

"Me neither really," he said.

He walked into the room and around the couch where he took a seat next to her. "Did you want to talk about it?"

Lilly thought about giving him the cold shoulder, but she knew she was better than that. "While what we did was nice, it can never happen again."

Morgan looked down at himself. "I was afraid you were going to say that."

"I'm sorry. It just wouldn't be fair to my son."

"I understand." Morgan nodded slowly.

They sat in silence for a brief moment. Neither knew what to say next. It was as if something held their tongues in place. Morgan looked to Lilly. He saw her mind working overtime as her eyes kept darting side to side.

"Let me make it up to you," he said. "Let's go out for breakfast. I'll pay."

"You don't need to make it up to me."

"I know that. I just want to show you that I'm okay with remaining friends over having a relationship."

"I believe you."

"I don't believe myself. I feel it'd be like a final test for me." Morgan smiled at her. "Can you do that for me?"

Lilly thought about it momentarily and then nodded.

"Great. Let's get changed and ready to go. I'll prepare a note for the others."

"A note?"

"Yes. I'll just write that we went out for breakfast because we were very hungry and for them to not have to fix a plate for us."

"*I'll* write that we went down to the market and are probably going to have breakfast," Lilly corrected him.

"Sounds perfect." Morgan got up and walked towards his bedroom.

Lilly sat for a short minute and then did the same. She entered her bedroom and put on her light burgundy Cheongsam dress and a pair of matching slides. She exited and found Morgan already standing by the door. He opened it and held it open for her.

"After you."

"Thank you," she said softly.

They got in the car and drove off.

The trip was a bit longer than Morgan anticipated. In that time, he grew fascinated with Lilly. As she handled the steering wheel with ease and the morning traffic with patience, there was a sense of admiration and respect she carried. He noticed it. She was not a fragile woman but one with confidence in herself. There were no angry outbursts at the cars that cut her off nor annoyance when pedestrians had to cross the street. It was admirable.

Soon, they were driving along the oceanside highway. It was not long until they found their destination. The car parked and they got out. The area ahead was wall-to-wall with markets.

Morgan noticed something right off the bat. "They're all on the water!"

"Yes."

"What about the crocodile?"

"Pieces of it were found yesterday."

Morgan sighed. "It's a shame they could not relocate it."

"I agree."

The two shared a smile. Lilly held out her hand and Morgan looked at it.

"It's very crowded in there. I don't want to lose you," she explained.

"Likewise." He could not help himself.

The two made their way down a set of steps and began their exploration of shopping on the sea.

Lilly passed by a few grocery markets. Her attention seemed to be focused ahead.

"What's wrong with these ones?" Morgan asked.

"They don't have what I need."

"What are you looking for?"

"Ribs. Spare ribs to be precise."

"Oh," Morgan said.

Eventually they came to a small area of the village, and she entered a little shop. Inside Lilly smiled at the familiar face. He welcomed them in Chinese, and she did the same. They then spoke the language which Morgan found to be fascinating. She then turned to him and gestured and spoke some more.

"Ah." The man's voice trailed off.

They then spoke a bit more. Morgan figured he was taking Lilly's order. He then gestured for them to sit at a table.

"Let's have breakfast while they prepare my order."

"Okay," Morgan said.

Both of them sat at a table right by the water. Morgan noted that, for it being a very populated area, the sea was particularly clear. He could almost see the bottom. "Nice place."

She saw him looking down at the water below. "Yes. Everyone tries to keep it nice and tidy."

Morgan then looked at Lilly. She smiled and turned away from him.

"I'm sorry. I can't help it," Morgan said.

"It's alright."

"No. It's not alright. I need to learn not to stare."

"Staring doesn't hurt."

"I can't control myself when I'm around you."

Lilly looked out at the market area. "Despite all the buildings, this is quite the beautiful place."

Morgan noted that there were faux trees everywhere giving the illusion that they were still on land. "It must have taken a long time to make it that way."

"Years." She turned back to him.

Morgan nodded.

"I wanted to be an actress once," Lilly started. "I even had an agent. He said I was good enough to be on television. Maybe even the movies one day. He promised me everything and then took it all away."

A single tear fell down her cheek. Morgan reached and grabbed a tissue from the dispenser. She accepted it.

"I'm sorry."

"You're fine," Morgan reassured her.

"I ended up pregnant. She was going to be a beautiful little girl." Her eyes wandered as if imagining what the child would have looked like. "One night, he came in drunk and beat me. By the time I got to the hospital, my baby was dead."

Morgan felt himself begin to tear up.

"The punk went to jail, and I married and had Yow. I divorced my husband because he was picking up drinking habits and becoming violent. Life just kept repeating itself." She stammered as she seemed to be choking on her own words.

"Well, at least you had Yow. He's a good guy. I've worked with him for a long time. I could tell that when I first met him though."

"He speaks the world of you too."

"Likewise." Morgan took a deep breath. "Lilly, I don't want you to live without a man. I don't want you to hurt again either."

"It's alright. I'm past my prime anyway."

"I don't believe that," Morgan chuckled.

"You're sweet." Lilly blushed.

Their eyes tried to look anywhere but at the other. They could not help it and kept finding each other.

"I think we should go." Lilly began to get up."

Morgan placed a hand delicately on hers. "Stay."

"Why?" she asked softly.

"Because I'm asking you to."

"Should you be?"

"I think so," Morgan smiled. "Do you?"

Lilly could not help it and gave into her desires, sitting back down at the table. "Yes."

Something felt right and then very wrong as a loud explosion could be heard somewhere in the village.

It was where the ocean connected to the waterway and village that the accident occurred. A boat was parting with the market area to fish for new supplies. It was a dinky watercraft but serviceable, nevertheless. Behind it was a canoe with two paddlers steering close.

Each fisherman in the area knew that the closer one got to the channel, the murkier the water appeared. It was all the soot and seaweed kicked up by the current.

There was a single fisherman in the first boat. He seemed to be enjoying the warmth of the sun as his engine propelled him further. He gave the occasional steer, but it was mechanics that brought him closer to the sea.

Suddenly, the boat went airborne with him in it. A geyser of water shot man and watercraft up like a rocket. Something below caused the wooden hull to splinter and crack. The two then plummeted back into the water. Everything but the man resurfaced. Instead, a continuous stream of blood bubbled up and flowed down to the channel.

The two rivermen on the boat began to scream and holler.

Across from them, sitting on the edge of a walkway near a hut, was an old man. He had seen a lot of weird stuff in his life. Strange fish with two heads of weird growths on their bodies. He had never seen anything like what he just witnessed.

The strange part was that neither he nor the two paddlers saw what caused the explosion of water and sea foam. It was as if Mother Nature had enough of engines and shot the man up. It was below that concerned them though.

Others began to notice. Villagers and shopkeepers alike came out slowly. It was not a quiet accident. Some whispered while others hollered, asking what happened.

Only one had the right demand.

"Get out of the water!" the old man cried.

There were other canoes coming upstream to join in the fishing brigade. Only a few up front saw the water spray from mere seconds ago.

Something that defied all logic and scale suddenly burst from the water. It had black and yellowish tan scales that were covered in barnacles. It rose so high it almost blocked the sun. It then came down with the force of a race car slamming into a wall. The two fishermen were helpless as it connected with their canoe, causing it to crack.

The old man blinked a few times as the massive tail of a crocodile came up again for another strike. This time, the canoe snapped in two as if it were a stick of butter.

"What the hell was that?" the old man cried. "Did everyone see that?"

Both fishermen surfaced and looked around. They saw the fate that befell their friend up ahead and were surprised they had even been given the chance to breathe again.

Turning to his right, the old man saw something startling. A wall of water was racing directly towards him. It was only then he realized his feet were dangling off the edge of the walkway. Before he could even react, a cavernous pair of jaws slammed shut on them. The crocodile did not even have to twist too sever them. They came off like a couple of Lego pieces.

Copious amounts of blood rocketed from the stumps and sprayed down into the water below where the two fishermen were. It acted as a seasoning to drive the crocodile's senses crazy.

It turned around after swallowing the legs and engulfed the two fishermen in one massive swallow.

The old man began to feel wheezy, and faint and he quickly fell into the water. He slowly sank and never resurfaced.

By this time, everyone was running around. Some were directionless, going as far as to run further into the village. Most were sensible enough to turn around and run for the exit.

There was a bridge on the right side facing the parking lot up ahead. It was built many years ago out of sturdy wood and strong rope. It could be filled to capacity and still hold an additional hundred pounds. In the moment of chaos and confusion, there were fifteen people trying to cross the ten-foot length of it. The mass exodus caused shoving and fear which, in turn, made the bridge sway left and right.

Some felt they were on a roller coaster while others were too scared to notice that the rod holding one side of the rope in place was creaking.

The once sturdy bridge was now becoming rickety. After a few minutes, some people began to slow, noticing the bridge getting closer to the water below.

"Stop!" a man with a goatee and thick set of black hair shouted.

A sudden lack of movement made him realize he had stopped another potential catastrophe. Soon, the bridge stopped swaying, and villagers began to take their time.

That all dashed away when the water began to churn beneath their panicking feet.

"It's going to get us!" a woman cried out.

Pushing and shoving, everyone tried to get off. It was too late. The crocodile's snout punched through the planks of wood and the bridge snapped in two. Multiple people fell into the water as the crocodile descended back down.

The first to go was the man with the goatee. He had surfaced first and was the closest towards a set of stairs that led up to the walkways.

They went straight down to the water and were partially submerged. He could feel the wood in his grip. He attempted to pull himself up but was quickly stopped and yanked back. He screamed loudly and there was a crunching sound. The battle was lost when he felt his fingers scraping against the wood as he was dragged away, leaving behind fingernails and streaks of blood. The crocodile then snapped its head to the left and let the man go. He was sent flying through the air until he came crashing through a thatched roof and onto a hot stove. His once drenched clothes quickly caught on fire, and he flailed about until he succumbed to the heat and unbearable pain.

As soon as he died, the hut he was in became engulfed in flames. The occupants were quickly scorched alive. Some took the risk and jumped into the water with the remaining people from the bridge.

It spread like wildfire, every hut nearby was either scorched or burnt. The crocodile's tail splashed around, crushing people. It seemed to know where to aim so it would not have water hit the huts and put the fire out.

Some people were lucky enough to make it onto walkways only to be knocked back in by the tail or collapsing infrastructures.

Others thought they were saved when they approached the channel. They would be swept out to sea but knew they could find their way to shore.

Then, something unexplainable happened. There was stirring in the water all around them. Several people were suddenly sucked down and whipped about. The force was so strong that most of their bodies snapped like twigs, their limbs going in unnatural directions.

"It's a whirlpool!" a man shouted.

Further up the canal, Morgan and Lilly saw the water from afar. It was a peculiar sight for there was no logical explanation for it. There were no fire hydrants around and no hose had enough power to cause such an explosion.

"What's happening?" Lilly had a concern in her tone that made Morgan worry.

Then the screaming began. A flock of people were running in their direction.

The table Morgan and Lilly were sitting at began to shake. They looked over the side and saw the water was not as clear as before. It was as if the sandy bottom was being dragged away.

"Let's get out of here," Morgan said and then grabbed Lilly by the hand. She did not resist.

Kaboom.

There was another explosion. It was so loud and deafening that everyone crouched down in reactionary defense. The shopkeeper quickly stood up and called for someone in the back. A young boy, roughly ten years old, came running from the kitchen. He ordered him to do something and the two then ran over to Morgan and Lilly. They helped them up and all four of them exited the market.

"What's happening?" Lilly called out in Chinese.

There was mostly screaming but, in the middle of the chaos, she heard the word *èyú* being shouted several times.

"What are they saying?"

Lilly turned to Morgan with a look of fear and disbelief. "Crocodile."

"No," Morgan said softly.

The shopkeeper and boy then grabbed both of them and pulled them away.

Morgan looked over his shoulder briefly and immediately wished he had not. The water level was so low, and the crocodile was so large. He could hear screaming coming from behind it as it rampaged up the canal.

Then, it stopped.

No one slowed as they ran. To the crocodile, it must have seemed like ants running away. At least, that's what Morgan thought. Then, without warning, there was a roar so loud that everyone screamed in response. It sounded like a guttural car engine. Afterwards, there was another sound. It was muffled but growing ever clearer, far away but coming quick.

Water blew around it as if the crocodile was projecting it towards them. It was a miniature tsunami that came barreling down on them.

Morgan quickly grabbed Lilly and ran inside a nearby shop. He then covered her with his body and silently prayed.

The water slammed down on the village, destroying most of the first half in mere seconds. Further down had already been ravaged by the crocodile. Soon there would be nothing left. Buildings were flooded instantaneously. Then, as quickly as it happened, it receded. The water level returned to normal but there was no one running anymore.

Before the crocodile was a smorgasbord. It continuously breached the surface with countless unconscious or injured people in its jaws. Each attack left more severed body parts than the last.

Morgan opened his eyes. They stung with saltwater but he was thankful he could still feel Lilly under him. Her arms were shivering as her dress was sleeveless. He looked around and saw the building they were in had barely any roof left. The whole front side was completely torn away giving him a perfect view of the carnage unfolding.

Lilly looked up at him and was grateful to see he was alive. She then saw the same things he did and wanted to scream but kept her composure. It was unlike any tragedy she had ever encountered before.

There was so much blood. It was practically raining down like a waterfall from the beast's jaws.

"Let's get out of here, now!" Morgan told her.

He helped her up and the two began to make their way out of the shop. They quickly noticed that, up ahead, the kid sat crouched next to the shopkeeper, crying. The man was unconscious.

Smoke was billowing out of a nearby structure. Morgan did not know why but he was not going to wait around to find out what would happen. He dragged Lilly over to them and assessed the situation quickly.

"Can you save him?" Lilly cried.

The man's head had a huge gash in it and his breathing was worrisome. "I can try but we have to get him to a hospital."

For a time, all was still. Morgan looked back and saw the crocodile was gone. It was not a dream. The thing was real and worse, it was still alive. He quickly scooped up the shopkeeper.

The walkway they were on suddenly shifted.

"It's working its way through the pilings!" Morgan shouted. "Let's go!"

Lilly aided Morgan with the shopkeeper while the boy stuck close behind them. Their waterlogged clothing slowed them for a brief moment but not long enough. Soon, their pace quickened, and they could even see the stairs up ahead.

"Oh, thank God," Morgan sighed with relief.

Soon they would be away from the water, get in the car and bring the man to the hospital. As far as Morgan was concerned, he would not be going anywhere near the ocean for a long time. The Chung's pool was calling his name.

He found the strength to pick up his speed. Lilly seemed to match him well. He kept his mind focused on the task at hand which was easy to do as a doctor and even easier when his and other's lives depended on it.

"Are we there yet?" the shopkeeper asked in Chinese.

"There you are," Lilly smiled.

She looked at Morgan and shared a smile.

They were only fifteen feet from the stairs now. A dozen more steps or so. They only made it half that distance before there was a cracking sound. Morgan turned back and saw the boy was not behind them anymore. In fact, half of the walkway was gone too.

"No!" he screamed.

Morgan relinquished the shopkeeper to Lilly and hurried over to survey the scene. The boy had not resurfaced yet. He silently prayed he would. He then turned back to Lilly.

"Get him to the car and stay there!"

"But…"

"Now!" he shouted at her.

She did not argue and helped carry the man up the steps one by one.

A gasp of air caught Morgan's attention. He looked back down and saw the boy had resurfaced and was now reaching for him. He extended his hands as far as they could go. They could not touch his. He then retracted, pushed himself up and forward and then tried again. He was practically hanging off the side by his waist.

It was then he felt the boy's slippery grasp around his hand, and he pulled him up so fast he did not even think if he would break his little arm.

Soon, they were both on the walkway. They sat on their rears and looked at the village. It was destroyed, potentially beyond repair. There were still limbs and gallons of blood in the water. It made the boy feel ill.

"C'mon. Let's go." Morgan picked him up and carried him towards the steps. Lilly was at the bottom of them, reaching out for the boy. He was about to hand him to her when the stairs suddenly shifted. Before anyone could react, Lilly fell into the water.

She quickly surfaced.

"Help me! It's going to get me!" she cried.

"I don't think it's close!" Morgan said as he reached down. "The whole area's falling apart. I think it's further down the…"

His relaxed expression soon turned into one of horror as the water came alive with teeth and gums and a fleshy mouth. Each tooth was nearly a foot and a half in length and the mouth seemed like an endless cavern of blackened horror.

Morgan fell backwards as Lilly let out a primal scream of fear. The crocodile rose and rose. Soon, it seemed its whole body was out of the water. Morgan could not help but notice all the gashes on its scales.

They had failed to kill it and now it was going to kill Lilly. He was about to get up and do something, what he was not sure. Her scream was prolonged, and she suddenly took a breath to bellow out in horror again. Before she could, the jaws snapped shut. She was encompassed in darkness. Feeling around, the tender flesh was disgusting, and the smell was pungent. There were other body parts in there with her.

She prayed the crocodile would open its mouth again. She had to escape. There was no way she could die now. She wanted to have a life with Morgan. To be happy with her son, daughter in-law, and granddaughter.

There was an awkward motion that propelled her further down its gullet. She was being swallowed and there was nothing she could do about it. The small amount of light that peeked in through the crocodile's teeth was now gone as was she.

CHAPTER FOURTEEN

The nightmare continued.

Things were different. The crocodile was still wreaking havoc, but Morgan was watching from the parking lot. He was far away from destruction but could still feel the warmth of Lilly's hand covering his own. He held her close and was able to smell her perfume. The sweet smell was fresh and exciting. Despite all they had been through, she still looked amazing as well. Her wavy black hair was just below her shoulders and her makeup was perfect.

She then mouthed the words, *I'll always love you.*

Something happened then. Chunks of hair began to fall from her scalp as her face morphed into a misshapen, gory mess. It looked as if it were melting away with some type of compound. He then realized what it was – stomach acid. She was melting away from the crocodile's bodily contents.

He reached out to grab her, to pull her away from the vile trap she was in, but she kept slipping away. He called out to her but no voice came out. His silent scream went heedless into the salty air. Then, as if the crocodile formed around her, blackness overcame them both. Blood rushed like a red wave towards him as it swept past Lilly and raced towards him.

Morgan shot up in the hospital bed. His screams could be heard from down the hallway. A pair of arms held him down as he cried and cried. Then, he let out one more primal bellow and collapsed.

His nightmare was not over. He immediately entered a world of blackness. There was no light, but he could smell the pungent stench of death. It was the crocodile's stomach, he knew it. He could hear Lilly calling his name. She sounded rather alert as if something were happening to him.

Suddenly, his eyes shot open. They darted around as he took in his surroundings. After a few intense deep breaths, he managed to find the words. "Oh God, Lilly."

Morgan's watery eyes ate into the Chung family before him. It was as if he answered a burning question they had been carrying for years.

"Grandma!" Dede whined aloud and then turned and cried in her mother's arms.

Yow tried to breathe but it came out rough. He felt as though he had been punched in the stomach. It was an invisible fist that knocked the wind right out of him.

"It can't be true," Sang said aloud, she herself finding it hard to speak.

Morgan did not respond.

"No," Yow said softly.

"I couldn't save her. Believe me, please oh please believe me!" Morgan tried to relax but found himself to be leaning so far that his hands could touch the guard bars at his feet.

At first, no one said anything. Then Yow spoke. "I believe you."

Morgan now felt like there was a brief moment of reprieve. He was able to breathe until he was thrust back into the memory of the look on Lilly's horrified face. It would stick with him for as long as he lived.

"I think you should return to America," Yow told him.

He nodded in response.

"I'm afraid I'm going to need a statement," a familiar voice to Yow said.

He turned and saw Sheriff Haruto Sans standing by the doorway. There was a nurse trying to sneak by him to inject Morgan with more sedatives.

"I'm sure you can gather from me what everyone else saw."

"That's just it, Mr. Stanley. Besides you, the boy, and the shopkeeper who is currently on life support, there are no witnesses."

"Everyone else is dead?" Morgan sat back on the bed in mild shock.

"I'm afraid so. We're estimating a total number of casualties in the sixties,   but   we   can't   be   sure."

Morgan slowly placed his hands on his face and sobbed.

"This isn't a good time," Sang told the lawman.

"I just have one question and then I'll leave you be." Haruto took a step further into the room. "Was it the crocodile?"

Feeling loopy as the nurse had already administered a light sedative, he recalled the creature in question. He nodded before drifting off.

"It's not dead," Yow said coldly.

"Not yet but my department has an idea on how to stop it."

"It's not possible I'd very much like to be a part of it, but I cannot," Yow said.

"I was hoping I wouldn't have to beg you," Haruto started.

"I would, but the answer is no. I need to be here for my family. I can't go around chasing monsters."

Haruto stood silent then shook his head. "I'd like you to at least advise the operation on land."

"I'm a doctor, Sheriff. Not a general or a military strategist." Yow turned away from him.

"Well, if you change your mind, we'll be on the Mai Po River come sunup."

"What's your plan, if you don't mind me asking?"

"I thought you wanted nothing to do with this operation," Haruto told him.

"Then I'm sorry I asked." Yow looked back at his daughter who was clutching her mother tightly. He brushed her hair and waited until the footsteps left the room and disappeared down the hallway.

***

The crocodile never went to its lair. The police waited there, guns in hand for hours each day. Sometimes until dark. The beast never returned. Kenji Ho, Pat, and Shu all accompanied Haruto to the rendezvous area where, if the officers needed to retreat, it would be their sanctuary. It was only a dry patch of land approximately one mile from the river. It would give them enough time to escape but the occasion never arrived.

Everyone felt defeated after the first day. By day three, there was no hope of its return.

All efforts were focused on the inlet, and nothing happened there, or out at sea. It appeared the crocodile was laying dormant for the time being.

"The damn thing's a coward!" Pat laughed one day.

"It's just recharging," Kenji told him. "I can assure you. It will attack   again."

"The damn thing was pissed that we blew it up. What happens when it finds out we're in its home?" Pat laughed nervously.

"I don't even want to know," Shu shuddered at the thought.

On one particular night, Kenji returned to his shack and broke several pieces of worthless furniture and a few lights that barely worked. His uproar went unheard, but he felt the crocodile could hear him. He was screaming at the sea, challenging it, beckoning for the surge of blood and waves to encompass him so he could laugh at the pain. It would be nothing compared to what he had gone through on Habito Island or since.

***

Morgan had been allowed to leave the hospital a day later. By that time, the Chungs were having Lilly's funeral. He did not miss it but kept his distance. He did not want to be noticed but failed.

Yow approached him from behind, startling him.

"Damnit, Yow! My heart can't take much more shock."

"Is that your medical diagnosis?"

He chuckled nervously. "It would be a serious loss to all hospitals around the world if I died of a heart attack."

The two shared a smirk.

"Look, Morgan. I don't blame you. It must have been a horrible thing to   see."

"It wasn't just that," he said.

"I know," Yow stated.

"What?"

"I could smell the melatonin in my water. I knew you two were up to something. It probably hurts even more for me to say this, but you would have   had   my   blessing."

Morgan choked a bit. "You're right. That hurt."

"Don't let it." Yow placed a hand on his shoulder. "She went through a couple of really bad relationships before. I believe you would have made her happy."

"I would have tried," Morgan sniffled.

"I know that, and she knew that."

"I feel like I could die and that would be alright," he said suddenly.

"That's just the pain talking." Yow patted his back. "Let's get back to the house."

"I thought you wanted me to leave?"

"I think you could use the company as much as we could right about now," Yow smiled.

***

Kenji Ho awakened the next morning to knocking on his door. He made his way down the creaking stairs and opened it. Before his eyes could adjust to the sun to see who it was, a woman's voice spoke.

"We have a new plan."

"Shu?" he asked, still groggy.

"May I come in?"

He moved out of the way and allowed her access to the messy area he called his living room.

"I apologize for the clutter."

"It's okay. I've been here before. Remember?" she chuckled.

"Right, right." Kenji nodded as he gestured for her to take a seat on an old chair.

She managed to sit on it without causing it to make a sound. He was inwardly impressed but his face showed no such recognition.

"What's this plan of yours?" he asked.

"It's something Ro came up with."

"Who?" he wondered.

"He's the deputy who got all the fishing boats together to go hunting for the crocodile."

"Ah, we see how well that idea turned out," Kenji scoffed.

"He was only following orders." Shu made a face. "Besides, he's young and has a wild imagination. Still, I think his idea is sound."

"How so?"

"Deputy Ro is to lead the expedition into the Mai Po River. He, along with several other deputies, will set up a razor wire perimeter around the only access point to the inlet where the crocodile lives."

"It hasn't returned there in days," Kenji laughed. "It's probably moved on."

"Pat doesn't think so. He's seen whales migrate and knows they'll eventually come back home. Plus, we have bait."

"What kind of bait?" Kenji asked.

"The humankind. We need fishermen to patrol the shoreline to look for the crocodile. When it's seen, they'll lure it with chum."

"Is that why you need me? For bait?"

"No. For your experience. Not only with fishing but from your encounter with this thing," Shu pleaded her case.

Kenji stood over her now. His breathing intensified. "I was lucky enough to escape that beast twice. I think the third time would be the charm but in the croc's favor."

"Please," Shu begged.

"There's no need for this. You hurt it with explosives before."

"We also lost a bunch of people. This operation should run much smoother."

"How so?" Kenji asked.

"We're not having them go out to fight it. They're out there to lure it home."

He backed away and made his way over to his door where he opened it. "I'm going to have to ask you to leave."

She stood up and marched over. "Please, think about it."

Kenji only nodded.

CHAPTER FIFTEEN

A time to relieve.

Morgan swam in the pool at the Chungs' house, doing backstrokes and staring up at the cloudless sky. He had been in there all day. His skin was liable to be pruned to the shape of a raisin. Occasionally, he switched positions and did some normal laps from one end to the other.

Sang stood at the sink doing dishes and watching him from the window. Yow had checked in on her a couple of times but her progress to finish the cleaning was slow. He could not blame her. He too was struggling with the loss of Lilly. It was only natural. She was his mother, and, in that, there was emptiness in the pit of his stomach.

Eventually, he came around to check in on her again. She was just finishing up and drying her hands with a rag. She looked up at him and forced a smile.

"I know. It's not going to be easy." He went over and hugged her.

"I just feel so lost," she replied. "I was planning on making lunch today and I had to keep reminding myself we didn't need a plate for her."

"There's so much I have on my mind. I can't understand why it happened, but it has. I'm trying to cope."

She wiped a tear from her eye. "You're doing better than me."

He kissed her forehead.

"Let's go out to eat. There's no need to be in this house today. There are too many reminders."

She nodded.

"Mommy!" Dede called out as she made her way into the kitchen. "I want to go swimming."

"No. Not today, sweetie." She tried to hide the idea of a monster roaming the shoreline. "We're going to go out to eat soon."

"But, Mom!"

"Listen to your mother," Yow ordered.

Dede turned and walked back to her room with her head hung low.

"I'll go get Morgan," Yow said as he left Sang to be with her thoughts for the time.

***

The wire was set. Most of the implementations were easy enough to secure. It was a dangerous operation, not only in planning but execution. Haruto was thankful none of his men had been cut by the wire.

They had crisscrossed it along the entrance of the canal. A couple of trees were chopped down and the wire was wrapped around them. The section on the trees was wrapped in a rubbery material that caused it to not rip through the stumps.

Haruto looked on with pride. He had managed to get a few steer carcasses from the local meat shop and they were being prepared with explosives. It was the backup plan he hoped would not have to be used. The wire ran for a good twenty feet across and in the water. It almost seemed too easy.

Shu had managed to acquire Kenji to aid in this operation. He and Pat were out on a boat, as were several other fishermen. They patrolled the shoreline, chumming with fish, blood, and whatever they found in the trash. It was a messy operation, but they were accustomed to it.

On the sidelines, Shu observed the area. The traces of the crocodile had all been dried up or misshapen. She hoped a croc carcass would be produced out of this. She needed a new purse and a pair of boots.

"How's it looking?" Haruto called out to Ro who was barking orders at a couple of the fellow deputies.

"We're all set over here."

"Don't let that control get to your head, kid," Haruto reminded him.

He gave a nod in response but clearly did not comprehend what he was saying. Everyone needed to be alert. Just because it looked flawless did not mean things would run perfectly. Things could go wrong very fast.

***

His eyes never left the water. He could sense it was near. The monster from the ocean floor. Despite all his pent-up rage at the creature, he was genuinely curious as to where it came from. As far as he could tell, it was the legend come to life. The vile crocodile was not born, nor did it come from any womb. It was given life through the stories. The fear it spread.

At least, that's what Kenji believed. Many others would chalk it up to bomb testing or genetic manipulation. Those were all good theories despite there being no real reason why it was able to control the weather.

"It's a god incarnate. I'm sure of it," Kenji said aloud.

Pat sat on the transom of Kenji's new fishing vessel, personally gifted to him by the mayor as promised. It was a nice boat. A real force not to be reckoned with. There was a short pulpit with a spear gun situated off to the right on the bow. The crow's nest was high off the deck and gave enough viewing range to spot any creature. On the stern were many utility boxes and a fighting chair. Kenji made it clear though it would not be used.

It was what was in the boxes that gave him more hope.

One case of dynamite complete with fuses, followed by the other containing a few machine guns.

Packs more punch than a small grenade. Kenji had laughed

Feeling more content on the fishing vessel, Pat began to look around. The cabin below was spacious but left little in the way of the comfortability department. It had room for several occupants but no cushioning on the sparse seats. The windows had no curtains to cover them either.

"You really need to spruce up this vessel," Pat called out to him.

"I'll hire a maid," Kenji scoffed at him.

"With what money?"

The captain shook his head in response. He felt like slapping his palm in his face but fought the urge.

As his frustration began to simmer, he reflected on the plan. It was straight up cartoonish in his opinion. There was no way it would work. The crocodile would stop just before the razor wire and avoid it like a plague. Its intelligence was way higher than anyone would have predicted. Kenji knew it though. He had known it for a year now.

"Starboard side!" Pat shouted suddenly.

The men looked off in the distance and saw a waterspout.

"It's just a whale," Kenji stated.

"No! It's not. I know what that looks like. This is less powerful. The crocodile must be exhaling it through its nostrils," Pat explained.

Kenji reached for the radio and altered the two other fishing boats in the area. One was a police vessel while the other was a fishing boat, albeit one on a much smaller scale than his.

They heard the boats approaching. Mayor Lee had closed the beaches and all water activities. Regardless, Kenji looked over his shoulder to verify the two watercrafts. When he looked back, he only saw one. It was the officer's.

"Where's the other boat?" he called down to Pat who was busy looking at the crocodile.

Now that they were getting closer, its scaly hide was becoming more visible, a prominent feature that stuck out of the water like a sore thumb.

"Pat!" Kenji yelled this time. "Where's the other boat?"

The coroner looked back and saw that it was indeed gone. Then he heard the screams.

Ahead, just behind the wall of scales, was the boat. The crocodile was in the process of tearing it apart.

"That was only its back!" Pat shouted in disbelief. "It's killing them!"

Kenji snapped into action and stopped the boat. They were close enough and he had to act swiftly. He raced towards the bow and loaded a harpoon into the cannon. Then, steadying his aim and inhaling, he took a shot.

The crocodile was in the process of eating the last fisherman when the projectile embedded itself in its soft underarm. It roared in defiance and then turned. Its gaze followed the trajectory, and he saw the fishing vessel.

Quickly inserting another harpoon, he did not have a chance to fire it. The boat suddenly turned to the left and began to maneuver away. Kenji looked up at the consol and saw Pat steering them away.

"What are you doing?" Kenji practically shrieked.

"You're just pissing it off!" Pat stated.

Bullets then whizzed past them. They both looked back and saw the police boat was charging for the crocodile. The rough waves made it hard for them to aim and their shots were way off.

"Turn back, you idiots!" Pat screamed at them.

They did not heed his warning.

By the time the boat was mere feet away from the reptile, Kenji was climbing up the ladder.

Pat turned to him. "We need to get it to the inlet. There's nothing we can do here to kill it."

Kenji did not respond. Instead, he noticed something on the shoreline. A little body was hopping up and down less than a mile away. It was a girl.

An explosion from the patrol boat made him jump. His reaction was hasty, but he punched Pat and knocked him onto the deck below. He then took control of the boat and steered towards the shore.

***

Morgan entered the home with a towel in hand as he brushed it through his damp hair. He walked towards the bedroom; the feeling of Lilly's nearness hurt. Her bedroom was so close to his. He recalled their night together, the tenderness of her touch and softness of her skin. It was exhilarating.

Now she was gone. He entered his own guestroom and began to change.

"Dede?" Sang called out.

He chuckled. Despite the current tragedy, Dede still managed to find the light in all of it. He figured she must be playing hide and go seek.

"Dede?" This time it was Yow. There was a hint of concern in his tone.

Quickly pulling his shirt over himself, Morgan opened the door and made his way out into the den where Sang was pacing back and forth.

"Where could she be?" she asked no one in particular.

"Did you guys check outside?" Morgan wondered.

"She knows better." Yow turned to Sang. "Right?"

Sang thought about it, reflecting on her own opinion of her daughter. She was normally obedient but did have a side of spunk she got from her grandmother. The thought of Lilly and what happened to her ran through her mind.

"Oh no," she said suddenly.

Everyone ran towards the sliding door at once. As soon as they were outside, Morgan ran to look over the pool. Despite the trick of the light on the deeper end which created some dark shading, there was no sign of an object in there.

Yow quickly opened the gate that fenced off the yard. He then began to circle the house at a quickened pace, his eyes darting towards every hiding spot she could possibly be in.

Sang too went through the gate and made her way down the grassy hill. Eventually, her feet touched sand. Ahead, there was a little beach towel and a bucket.

There was then a muffled explosion off in the distance, but she paid it no mind.

"No," she said coldly.

The items were clearly hers. At first, Sang did not want to look at the ocean. She was afraid she would see her daughter's unconscious body idling in the surf.

"Dede!" she screamed.

"I'm over here, Mommy!" Dede called to her.

Further down the beach, she sat in the low tide, her little bum bouncing in the waves. Sang would not have thought of looking over there, it was on their neighbor's property. They lived on an even steeper hill than their own that went out over the water. Dede was almost beyond the point of view.

Sang began to run over when there was a sloshing sound. Dede's head then snapped upward, and she screamed. She was looking at something just beyond the hill. Sang hurried over and saw something that almost caused her to freeze in fear. Her paralysis was only overcome by the need to protect her daughter.

There, standing in four feet of water, with its massive head covered in scales and barnacles, and its short legs that allowed it to creep closer and closer, was the crocodile. Sang could not believe how large it was. It was abnormal.

"Dede," she stammered.

Her daughter did not respond. She was transfixed by the great predator.

"Don't move." The words registered in her head, but she could not fully comprehend them.

The jaws parted and a deep, cavernous mouth appeared before her. Its smell was appalling, the guttural growl was deceptively soothing. It was almost as if it were calling her closer.

Yow and Morgan came down the hill but stopped halfway. The look on Sang's face alone was concerning.

She then noticed them and looked at them with pleading eyes.

"What is it?" Yow asked.

Quiet.

The two then continued down the hill until they were touching sand. They then trudged towards her. They followed her gaze and had a similar reaction to when she first saw it.

A dozen yards away, Dede sat still while the crocodile crept closer. Yow took a step forward, ready to charge, when Morgan stopped him. The sound of a boat engine was growing ever closer.

He then pointed. "Look!"

Neither took their eyes off Dede and the crocodile but there was indeed a large vessel coming into shore. It was aiming right for the crocodile.

"Damnit! How did it get there so fast?" Kenji shouted in anger.

A defiant rage stirred within him. The crocodile was too fast. He was surprised he had even hit it with the harpoon before. It was like it was teasing the idea that he could stop it.

Now it was different though. It seemed to be taking its time on shore as it approached the little girl. It was savoring the moment.

"You damn devil!" Kenji cursed.

A moment of rational clarity came to him. If he destroyed his ship, he would not be able to lure the crocodile to the trap. There had to be another way. He looked down at Pat who was still unconscious. Giving him a couple of kicks to his sides, he tried to rouse him. It did not work.

"Get up!" Kenji yelled.

He then gave a swift kick to his ribs which sent his hands quickly down to his side. Then the pain rushed to his head. He groaned loudly. "Oohh, what did you do?"

"I need you to man the harpoon gun. There's a spear still in it. We're closing in on the crocodile!"

"We're what?"

Kenji looked up. They were close.

"Change of plans. Just hold the steering wheel in place. You can stay on the ground."

The coroner did so with a weakened grip. His strength was slowly coming back but it was still taxing on his body to keep ahold of the wheel.

Without a second to lose, Kenji slid forward down the ladder and quickly climbed around the starboard side. Soon he was at the bow. He grabbed the harpoon and aimed.The trajectory of the harpoon had to be just right. It would have to go past the little girl and directly into the crocodile. He was not certain he could penetrate it but it would get its attention no doubt.

He said a silent prayer, focused his shot to match directly in line with the crocodile, and fired.

Morgan watched as the projectile launched from the cannon. He held his breath. Yow and Sang were both a few feet ahead of him. They were slowly making their way to their daughter. He wanted to call out to them, to let them know the fishing boat would stop it but decided against it.

The harpoon whizzed past Dede's head and hit directly into the crocodile's open mouth, embedding itself on the roof of its jaws. It let out an otherworldly roar and began to writhe around.

Dede looked on at the awesome sight before her. She then felt weightless as she felt her father's hairy arms wrapped around her. He pulled her back. Sang was nearby.

The crocodile then spun its massive girth in place. It rolled around, the wire attached to the harpoon swinging like a jump rope. It caught Sang by her feet and caused her to trip over it.

"Mommy!" Dede cried out as she looked in horror.

Morgan ran towards Yow who handed him Dede. He then turned around and made his way towards Sang.

She was slow to get back on her feet. The sound of a cable snapping scared her, and she fell back to the ground. She then managed to get back to her feet just in time to see the crocodile recover from its scratch.

Without thinking, she turned to run. Yow was close but the crocodile was closer. It charged for her just as an explosion went off on its left side.

Yow fell to the ground. The impact was direct, but he did not believe it killed the crocodile. He hoped it did, but there were doubts. He got up as the smoke began to clear. The crocodile was gone and Sang was on the ground. He ran to her, several questions running through his mind like rapid fire. *Where's the crocodile? Is Sang hurt? Is my wife still alive?*

Before he could find out answers to his wife's health, he heard a roar. It was pained. He saw the crocodile in the water as it raced after the boat. He saw Pat steering with Kenji firing at it with a machine gun.

He soon knelt down next to Sang and looked her over. She seemed alright... until he turned her around. Half her face was burnt, and chunks of her hair were missing. The side of her body was singed. Her arm slowly raised and he saw her left hand was missing.

Yow screamed in horror. He could not believe it. She was severely injured. His cries were a mixture of pain and anger. His mind tried to understand what he was seeing. He then looked over his shoulder at Morgan and Dede.

"Call an ambulance!" His tone was that of a distraught but hopeful man.

Morgan quickly ran towards the house.

***

Their patience was growing thin. The swampy area and sweltering heat were beginning to bother the deputies, something fierce. A couple of men, donning wetsuits, were especially miserable. Beads of perspiration poured down their faces. One man, with shaggy black hair, was even breathing through his mouth.

Haruto stood on the right edge of the mouth of the inlet. Originally, he was to wait further inland, but he realized he could not bear the thought of allowing his men to fight this great predator while he stood on the sidelines.

Shu stood on the left side of the bank with the same mentality. Despite not being part of the force, she was in the same department as the rest. The situation grew more into a communal affair. Everyone wanted to help as well as take a crack at killing the crocodile.

Everyone had been relatively silent up until that point. It made the sound of the engine approaching all the more audible.

"They're coming!" Haruto hollered over his shoulder.

Deputy Ro, with his wetsuit and long shaggy hair was excited. Normally getting into a swamp would not entice him. Getting out of the heat outweighed the reluctance. He could not wait to see the sliced-up carcass.

The mountain of water that sprayed behind the fishing boat was enough to make some of the officers second guess their predicament. It was practically up against the stern, charging at a speed that seemed impossible for an animal of such size. It also seemed to not be tiring. The animal probably could go faster but, instead, was toying with Kenji and Pat.

Turning hard to port, the boat's hull rubbed against the sandy bottom. It soon found open water again and began to speed towards the inlet entryway.

Ro had thought about everything. The wire was low enough to not capsize the boat, yet high enough to slice open the crocodile's belly if it tried to climb over. It ran all the way to the bottom so there was no way it could maneuver around it.

Shu and Haruto ran back from the mouth of the inlet and over to Ro who looked ecstatic. It would all be over soon.

Kenji drove the boat in, the reptile hot on his trail. There was a sudden explosion of water. The frothing substance was not only yellow white but red. The crocodile had hit the razor wire full force.

"Destroy that!" Ro laughed as he grabbed for his snorkel.

The other man, a reporter, reluctantly did the same.

"Alright, let's get in there and capture the damage. I want to do this fast before the water gets too messy," Ro laughed.

Both men trudged into the water. The reporter had a special, underwater video camera. It was the same kind used to make movies with. His editor had been gracious enough to provide him with it given the murkiness of the water.

Meanwhile, Pat climbed down the ladder. His jaw was swollen, and he was clutching his ribs. He wanted to deck Kenji in the face but decided against it. The two then got off the boat and walked over to Haruto and Shu.

"I guess it's finally over?" Shu hoped.

"I'll believe it when I see it," Kenji stated.

CHAPTER SIXTEEN

It was part of the job.

Murkiness clouded their vision as they descended down the drop off. Ro was not used to such dirty water but was too excited to find the mangled monster that he did not really care. The reporter was a bit spooked. He failed to mention to anyone that he had a case of thalassophobia, but it was not that serious. He knew he still had a job to do and took it more seriously than some dark, dank water.

Blood clouds soon began wafting towards them, swirling in the brown around them. The red substance began to grow thicker, indicating the crocodile was near.

Ro looked over at the reporter and motioned for him to come closer. He reluctantly did so. Up ahead, there were signs of distress given that mud had been kicked up. Soon, they saw it. The large black mass. It was entangled in the wire. Lacerations covered its snout. Some of the slices ran down the side of its lower jaw. It looked like it had turned to dodge the oncoming trap.

There was a sudden doubt in Ro's mind. The crocodile looked dead, unmoving, swaying, yet its eyes seemed to stare daggers at him. Then there was a sudden flash of light.

The deputy looked back and saw the reporter flashing away at the crocodile. Ro wanted to stop him but realized there was nothing he could do. There was no way to speak to him. He could grab the camera, but he wondered if the crocodile was dead or alive. If it was dead, there was no reason to stop him. If it were alive though…

A muffled clicking sound came followed by another flash.

This time, Ro could have sworn the crocodile moved. It had happened right after the flash, while his eyes were still adjusting. He wondered if his eyes were playing tricks on him.

You're worrying too much. The damn thing's dead, he told himself.

Movement caught his attention again. This time, it was a single rock falling down a few feet from them. It landed in the water with a thud. Ro watched it fall and then turned back to the crocodile. It was beginning to move.

No!

The reporter suddenly abandoned his expensive high-tech camera and darted for the surface. Ro remained there motionless. His plan had failed.

"Get out of the water!" Shu yelled to the reporter.

"Where's Ro?" Haruto asked.

The reporter paid him no mind as he began to swim towards shore. His front stroke was a bit clumsy, but he was making progress unlike Ro who was still beneath the surface.

"I'm going in after him," Haruto stated as he began to pull off his boots.

"Don't!" Pat said. "There's no need to get both yourselves killed."

He ignored him.

"We have to stop him!" Shu exclaimed.

Haruto was about to trudge into the water after his deputy. Kenji took a step towards him when the sound of snapping wire could be heard.

Ro was amazed by the sheer size of the crocodile. It was enormous. The jaws alone were half the length of the inlet entrance. Which, after having measured them to put the razor wire in, was a twelve-foot gap.

Then, suddenly, something entered the water. He turned to look, expecting to see other officers coming to his aid. Instead, a large object came charging towards him from his left. It smashed into him at full force.

"Oh my god!" Shu screamed.

The wires cut through the stumps, sending flakes of splintered wood and uprooted dirt flying into the air.

A couple of the officers tossed more rocks into the water to get Ro's attention. Their attempts seemed to be in vain though.

"It's going to get him!" one of them shouted.

Kenji grabbed Haruto by the shoulder. "There's nothing we can do for him."

The sheriff looked at him with a blank expression.

"How the hell did it survive that?" The reporter climbed onto the shore. He spoke in between exasperated breaths.

"You left him!" Haruto reached down and pulled the man off the ground.

"I was scared!" he pleaded.

"The crocodile!" Shu pointed. "It's free!"

"Everyone get away from the water!" Kenji shouted.

Haruto relinquished the reporter who fell down into the mud. He then turned and his face went from rage to disbelief. The massive reptile was racing towards the shore.

Ro felt the wind knocked out of him, along with his regulator. He felt around for it, desperately searching for that sweet oxygen. His lungs were burning now. He could not locate the device. It seemed like every time he thought he had it, it would end up being seaweed or a stick. There was a sense of relief when he finally felt it in his grip. He placed it back over his mouth and observed his surroundings.

It was not too hard to figure out that one of the stumps that the wire was attached to had been yanked out of the ground and into the water. He was now trapped under it. He tried to dig but with every attempt the mud would settle back into place.

He groaned as he tried to lift the stump. He would need a crane to get it off it. Eventually he gave up. Tired from the exertion his effort caused, he realized he was stuck indefinitely without aid.

Swoosh.

Something massive rushed by him. He felt the stump get caught up in the current. It was now or never. He decided to try one last time in a desperate attempt for survival. He dug his fingers into the mud and pushed up. Miraculously, his legs were free. He let out a sharp exhale and then looked around. The crocodile was now climbing ashore. He could see its tail leaving the water.

He could not fathom how or why he was alive. The crocodile had inadvertently saved him. There was cause for rejoice. Was he given a second chance at the claws of a god? That was what Kenji referred to it as, a god incarnate. There was not much time to reflect. He pushed himself off the bottom and felt sudden pain. He looked down and saw a bone sticking out of his leg.

It's broken!

Holding it, he began to panic. There had to be a way to the surface. Instinctively, he used his arms to help him to the top where the summer sun shimmered along it.

Pat observed the crocodile. While he knew more about whales, he figured reptiles could not be too much different than mammals, especially at this one's size. It was struggling to climb ashore, its weight constantly holding it back.

Everyone backed up. No one abandoned their post. Some of the officers even raised their service rifles to fire at it if it attempted to come on land.

It kept grunting. Its low growl was wet as if it were choking on phlegm or plasma. There were lacerations all over its face, but they were not deep enough to cause any fatal injuries.

"Unless you're all waiting for this thing to die of an infection, I suggest everyone back away," Kenji stated.

"It can't possibly get ashore," Pat said.

"Tell that to Kowloon Dairy," a random officer in the crowd stated.

The reporter suddenly stepped in front of them all. He took it slowly, each step making squelching sounds in the mud. He raised another camera he had tucked away in a pouch on the beach.

"I don't think that's a good idea," Haruto suggested.

He ignored him as the crocodile's mighty jaws opened.

"Smile for the camera, big boy," he chuckled.

Kenji turned away and began to trudge back up the bank. Shu began after him. He then stopped and turned. There was no flash. He thought there could be something wrong with the camera. The sight that was bestowed upon him was one of horror. The reporter was still there except his knees were buried in the mud. Everything above his midsection was gone.

As the rest of the body fell down, intestines poured out into the water. Everyone began to fire at the beast as it quickly made its way up onto the sand with no issue whatsoever.

Each shot fired bounced off its scales as if they were Tic Tacs. It attacked the first thing it could get its jaws on. Pat. He was shaken with the ferocity of a dog playing with a chew toy.

"No!" Shu began to go back over to help.

Kenji grabbed her by the arm and forced her to run away with him.

Several officers continued to fire while the rest fled. The crocodile opened its mouth wide, as if urging them to keep shooting, allowing each shot to penetrate the inside of it. It then clamped down on three officers who were too sure of themselves and got too close.

Two other officers backed away but continued shooting. One of them aimed for the eye while the other under the belly. Its nictating lense quickly slid over its eye to protect it.

"What is this damn thing?" Haruto screamed.

The two officers were not aware how fast it could lunge at them. It struck them with the force of a freight train. One of them flew back into a tree, his body broken and destroyed. The other was lucky enough to barely survive the impact. He landed in a soft patch of dirt. He could only move his right arm. The other was broken. He struggled to climb forward. Every inch of progress he made, he seemed to sink into the earth. He cried out, realizing his predicament.

Haruto saw him and ran to help him. By the time he was able to reach him, he was already three quarters into the pit. They locked hands but the sheriff's upper body strength was not enough to hoist him onto the shore. He was reaching over the quicksand, there was nothing he could do.

A sudden roar caught his attention, and his head snapped in its direction. The noise was so intense. He reached to cover his ears but realized he had also let go of his deputy. By the time he reached again, he was gone.

"No!" he cried.

He looked over at the crocodile on the shore. It was eyeing the deputies off in the distance. It hunched down and then propelled itself with extreme force, off the ground, into the air. It landed directly in the path of the fleeing officers.

Their feeble attempts to shoot at it ended swiftly as it scooped them up in its jaws. All six deputies disappeared down its gullet with a slimy swallow.

Haruto felt faint. He saw the crocodile as it reared its head and let out one mighty roar and then made its way deeper into the swamp.

There was no telling where it was going next.

PART THREE:
THE HUNT

CHAPTER ONE

Something to dread.

Haruto sat in his office with a grim expression. In all his years of being on the force, he had never encountered anything like what happened out in that swamp. He knew the risks, as did his men. Now, fifteen of them were dead and their badges were spaced evenly on his desk.

The only officer to make it out was Ro and he was badly injured. Shu and Kenji were lucky enough to run in the opposite direction of the others. The crocodile had leapt at them with the agility and ferocity of a cat.

Questions filled Haruto's mind. *Why was this thing here? Where did it come from? How could it do these things?*

It haunted him to his very soul. Eating away at his mind as his heart went out to his fallen men. The attempt at stopping this beast had failed spectacularly.

He then thought of Pat. The poor coroner did not deserve that fate. He had offered to go out and help them because he was good at fishing and understood, to some extent, sea life. Even though his knowledge was mostly based in whales, he still proved helpful. Now he was just a ragged piece of meat being scooped up by another coroner.

There was a knock at his door.

Haruto looked up to see Kenji. He was a bit taken aback by his presence. The man liked to keep a low profile but was helpful in trying to stop the crocodile, even if the attempt had failed.

"What can I do for you, Mr. Ho?"

"Sheriff. Firstly, I want to apologize."

"Apologize?"

"My attempt at luring the crocodile was successful yet proved to not be enough to stop it."

"No apology needed. However, that does not undermine the fact that we still need a plan to stop this thing."

"I understand," Kenji said. "Maybe we can try another direct attack? This time with more dynamite? I was thinking of attaching some to the harpoons this time."

"I fear it may be more difficult than that." Haruto took a deep breath. "I'm considering getting in touch with a Hong Kong military base."

"You know someone there?"

"A general."

"Can he be useful?"

Haruto inhaled again. "I don't see any other option."

"What's his name?"

"General Sands." Haruto reached for his phone. "I guess I'd better get ahold of him now before there's another massacre."

"Wait!" a man's voice came from the hallway.

Both of them looked to see an unkempt man running towards the office. He was unshaven and looked like he had not slept for two days. He stopped before Kenji and looked at him. His expression was one of hate and respect.

"Can I help you?" Kenji asked.

The man clenched his fist, struggling to fight the urge to knock his lights out.

"Yow, don't." Haruto stood up at his desk.

"You almost killed my daughter." Yow's voice shook with rage.

"What?" Kenji was taken aback.

"But then you saved her. While at the same time burning my wife."

"I..." Kenji thought back. "I'm sorry. I did not intend to do such a thing. I was trying to stop the crocodile."

"If you had better aim you would have not injured my wife."

"If I hadn't taken the shot your wife would be dead," Kenji argued.

Yow inhaled sharply.

"Gentlemen. Please. Take a seat. There's no need for fighting over this," Haruto said calmly.

The staring competition ended when Kenji slowly made his way over to the chair. Yow soon did the same but did not take his eyes off the fisherman.

"Why are you here, Mr. Chung?"

He had to tear his gaze away to look at the sheriff. "I have a plan."

"Oh?"

"It's a bit risky but it might work."

"Is that so?" Haruto's eyebrow arched.

"I heard this crocodile is heading back out to sea, yes?"

"The scouters have reported sightings of it returning to the bay," Haruto confirmed.

"We need to get it away from any reefs or coral beds in order not to affect the environment."

"What are you proposing?" Kenji asked.

There was a pause.

"This creature is still vulnerable to conventional weaponry. It can be stopped. I think if we poison it though, we'd have greater results."

"You want to make a gargantuan crocodile sick?" Kenji scoffed.

"I don't see any other way of taking it out." Yow turned to him. "Do you?"

Kenji thought back on all the failed attempts. He wondered if poisoning it would be the way to take it out. Or at the very least weaken the behemoth.

"What do we need?"

"Strychnine. Lots of it. We have some at the hospital," Yow explained.

"Why would you have strychnine at the hospital? "Kenji asked.

"It can be used towards strengthening muscle contractions. Everything from hearts to bowel stimulants can be affected by it."

"Great. So, the croc will shit itself to death," Haruto chuckled.

"Well. It's only meant to be taken in small doses. Once the expulsion begins, it will draw other fish. Hence why I want to keep it as far away from those areas as possible."

"Why?" Kenji already had a feeling he knew the answer.

"Because it can infect the water they flow through their gills or the food, in this case excrement, they ingest."

"Lovely." Haruto sat back in his chair.

"It's either this or let it continue to terrorize Kowloon until it moves onto bigger areas. My friend thinks it's testing the waters, so to speak," Yow said.

"How does your friend know this?"

"Because, before he studied for his doctorate, he was big into herpetology."

"Herpetology?" Haruto inquired.

"The study of reptiles," Yow stated.

"I see." Haruto leaned forward. "Is this friend of yours around?"

"He doesn't need to be a part of this. He lost someone he cared about to the crocodile."

"I feel that'd be all the more reason for him to come along," Kenji chimed in.

Yow glared at him. "I'm not offering his services. If he wants to go, that'd be up to him."

"Bring him by the harbor tomorrow. I'll convince him," Kenji stated.

"I don't think he'll need much prompting," Yow said softly.

***

There was a sullen tone in Morgan's voice as he mumbled in his sleep. Yow had entered the house to see him sleeping on the couch. It was midday and all the curtains were open. Still, Morgan found a way to pass out despite the sun beating aggressively on his face.

Yow was not sure if he should wake him. There were times to awaken someone from a nightmare and others, from a dream. He could not tell which Morgan was having. There was a sense that he was making amends with someone. Possibly asking for forgiveness. Yow had a pretty good idea who it was.

The very thought of his mother being gone had not caused him to drop to his knees in tears yet. Part of him believed she was still alive. That what happened was not concrete. Sang had survived. Why could Lilly not? He found himself thinking a lot about what happened. Indeed, Morgan's experience was horrible. Yow began to wonder if he could have done more.

He then thought about himself. Had he been more out in the open with his feelings towards her and Morgan's relationship, they may never have even gone to the market. Even then that did not make him feel better. She most likely had better chances with Morgan than alone.

More ideas came swimming into his mind. *If I had not been so stubborn, maybe my mother would not have been afraid to tell me about her and Morgan. Am I a bad son? Was I a bad son? Am I still a son or is that title now stripped away?*

"Mommy," he then muttered uncontrollably.

His legs began to wobble.

It cannot be. You're not gone. You've suffered too much. You were going to be happy. Now you're gone.

He placed his hands on his face and began to sob. He then walked awkwardly over to the bathroom and tried to wash up. He was glad Dede was not here to see him like this. One of the nurses offered to put her in a daycare program until her mother was able to see her.

"I can't." Yow pulled his shaking hands away from his face and looked at them. "I can't believe she's gone."

"Me neither," Morgan said.

Yow spun around to see him standing by the bathroom door. The two men regarded each other with shame.

"How can life be so cruel?" Yow asked.

"I can't answer that," Morgan said, his nose congested.

Yow looked around the bathroom for a towel. He reached for the one to wipe hands with and patted his face with it. "I'm sorry."

"About what?" Morgan said, teary eyed.

"I should've come forth with my opinion on you two a lot sooner."

"It would not have stopped us from going to the market. The crocodile would have attacked whether you approved or not," he stated.

Yow nodded. "It's going to keep happening to other people if we don't stop it."

"Do you have a plan?" Morgan asked.

"That depends. Are you still knowledgeable on reptiles?"

"I wouldn't even have to bring a book on them," he said with some optimism.

"Then yes. I have a plan."

***

Mako had returned to his chief editor with a dour expression. He had given the photos to the authorities first rather than the paper. When he had entered the office, the bigwig in journalism asked why he had looked so upset.

It was the total opposite reaction he was expecting. Instead of disappointment or an egregious outburst, he put a bundle of cash held together with a gold clip on the table.

He was then told to hire a boatman to take him out there and find the fishing boat that was chased by the crocodile the day of the plan. Mako did not understand at first. His boss then went into detail, telling him he had been reported to that they were loading up for another planned hunt.

Now he sat at his desk in his living room. He was told the pictures were crap and could not be used anyway. Hence why he sent Tao to take pictures of the second attempt to kill the creature. It cost him his life. It made Mako reconsider his position at the paper.

It was not until he received word that the crocodile was officially back out at sea that he began to reconsider. The swamp was marshland, hard to work with and walk in. The open sea might prove easier to finish the beast off.

The first plan was similar. An oceanic battle that resulted in several lives being taken by the crocodile. He had asked what was different about this mission and he was informed of a one Yow Chung and Morgan Stanley accompanying the sheriff and Kenji Ho on the mission. It added a level of scientific authority that made him realize there may be hope after all.

Slowly taking a sip of tea as he looked at the wad of cash, he simmered. It was half gone; the boatman had been acquired. He was paid half in advance and half upon delivering him to the boat. The plan was in motion.

***

A glow so bright it shimmered under the water. A pod of white dolphins was making their way up the coastline of Kowloon's Victoria Harbor. Several boats steered clear of them. It was a great risk to hit whale in Hong Kong and the fines added salt to the wound.

There were four of them, darting left and right under the surface. They seemed to be moving in an erratic manner, but no one knew why. Some did not even notice their strange behavior. Others did and took note of it. It looked like something was chasing them.

Gushing water frothed and sprayed in the distance. Several boaters looked out and saw a massive girth roll in the water. It was like it was playing peekaboo with the dolphins or scouring its next meal.

Engines started quickly. Most were already on the move while the others were puttering along. The only similarity between them all were the shouts and screams.

The moonlight cast an ominous gloom over them. They were directly in its ray of light. It was as if Mother Nature herself was pointing them out for the crocodile to find easier.

It took no more than thirty seconds for the crocodile to cover the distance. It smashed into boats that were immediately capsized. Their occupants were either devoured, drowned, or brushed aside by the massive girth of the reptile. They all feared it would come back for them, so they frantically darted for the upturned hulls.

A gargantuan tidal wave soon followed the crocodile. It came in with a roaring rush of water that smashed into the faster vessels. The harbor was soon a waterway of waste and wounded.

Four dolphins, fleeing for their lives, looked back and saw the damage the crocodile had made. They wanted to aid the humans, give them a ride to shore. There was no way to get to them without putting their lives at risk. Instead, they continued out to sea. The crocodile soon gave chase.

CHAPTER TWO

Grave consequences.

News of the crocodile attacking the harbor had reached Haruto mere minutes after. He, along with Shu, were allowed onto the beach while dozens of onlookers silently watched. There was no commotion from the crowd. The reptile was public knowledge at this point. Everyone mourned the loss of the boaters.

Haruto stood on the beach, looking out over the water. His mind was elsewhere, as if lost in some cosmic void of horror. Shu, meanwhile, scoured the area for wreckage. She, herself, needed to understand how the crocodile attacked. She had ordered steel frames for Kenji's boat but, a tooth would go a long way as to how thick it needed to be.

She soon found herself nearing Haruto. She gave him a meaningful pout. The man was clearly distraught. He did not acknowledge her presence. In fact, he did not move an inch.

"Are you okay?"

There was a sign of a nod from him but not much else.

"Listen. The parts will come in soon and then you and the others can go out and end this."

"We need to leave sooner," he stated.

"I know. There's only so much that can be done."

"We've done enough already." He glanced at her. "Humans, that is. I'm not of the opinion this is some god. Kenji is crazy. It's probably from nuclear barrels dropped in the sea."

"Did you test for radiation?" Shu asked.

"No. But we will."

"No need. I already did."

He looked to her fully now. "And?"

"Clean. This is just a gargantuan creature of unknown origin."

"It's a crocodile," Haruto said flatly.

She shook her head. "It's not just any crocodile. It's prehistoric."

"What do you mean? Like it's a dinosaur or something?" Haruto chuckled.

"I wouldn't be surprised."

"Where did it come from then? Why haven't we seen it until now?"

"I'm not sure," Shu continued. "Our oceans are massive. They stretch for hundreds of thousands of miles and run deep. Who's to say some great predator couldn't have come to the surface."

"Sure. Next, you'll tell me a mammoth shark will breach the waters and wreak havoc. Or some kind of Kraken."

"Giant squid are real," Shu smirked.

"Don't be cheeky," Haruto said sullenly.

"Yes sir!" She turned to leave. "Oh, and just so you know. I believe it may or may not be a god. There is one thing it is though."

"What's that?"

"A miracle."

"Ha. You're crazier than Kenji."

"I felt like you'd say something like that."

***

The patience for the parts was eating away at Haruto. It had been two days. He began to wonder if he should go pick them up or if they'd even arrive at all. He found himself pacing in his office on a daily basis.

Amidst the concern, his men were growing restless. The crocodile had not attacked any other area in the last fifty hours. Still, there was a chance it was biding its time.

Yow entered his office with his friend who looked equally as distraught.

"Mr. Stanley?" Haruto extended his hand.

Morgan nodded and accepted the gesture.

"I assume Yow has informed you of the plan."

"Yes."

"What are your thoughts on it?"

"I think it needs to be tweaked. Yow disagrees "

"Tweaked? How so?"

"He believes we should load up a cow with poison to use as bait."

"That seems more of a direct attack."

"It's not," Yow continued. "You put a steer in the water loaded with strychnine and every little nibbler in the area will have a taste."

Haruto sat back in his chair and contemplated.

"Sheriff, if I can get a direct hit in the crocodile's mouth with the harpoon, there will be no reason to pollute the water."

"What of the crocodile itself?" Haruto folded his hands on his lap.

"What do you mean?"

"I mean that if the crocodile is loaded up with strychnine and we blow it to all hell, wouldn't sea life gorge on that too?"

Yow sat silently.

"Then we don't blow it up," Morgan stated. "We inject it with the poison and then get the hell out of there. We'll have a dredger pull the carcass back in before it pollutes the area too much."

"What if that thing is hot on our tails?" Haruto asked.

"The effects of the poison shouldn't take more than ten minutes to take effect."

"We could all be dead in ten seconds."

"Then what do you suggest?" Yow wondered.

"I suggest that we at least have a plan B in case everything goes to hell."

Morgan looked from Haruto to Yow. "We can implement my plan if all else fails."

"What's your plan, Mr. Stanley?"

"It's similar to Yow's. Except we won't need the poison. We'll use what's left of the razor wire as a net and then blast it to all hell while it's trapped."

"Too risky," Haruto said.

"You wanted a backup. However, I'd suggest making it plan A given that the poison could get in the water if we blow it up."

"Alright." Haruto nodded. "I'll have my men gather the razor wire. Maybe Kenji can fashion it into a net."

"Then it's settled," Yow had a hint of annoyance in his tone.

"I'm all ears if you have another plan, Mr. Chung."

He shook his head.

"The metal framing for the boat should be in any day now. We'll put everything together. I plan to leave sometime this weekend."

"Hopefully the crocodile can wait that long," Yow mumbled.

***

A reflection of a time long ago filled Kenji's mind as parts for the ship came rolling on the back of trucks. He had flashbacks to when his village had built huts and the trial, error, and effort put into them. Everything was easier here. The long steel frames were lowered into the water and then jacked up against the hull. Then, they were welded on with torches. Each one took a while. Still, Kenji found himself lost in thought.

He puffed on his cigarette and watched the process being completed with ease. He huffed at the thought. His people took such pride in their work. These men were only doing a job, a gig. There was no honor in what people were doing for work these days.

Shu came up and stood next to him. The harbor had a pleasant view. The opening channel was wide so that big ships could enter. Horns honked frequently. Yet, with all the commotion, it was easy to get lost in the lapping waves. The calm, rhythmic motion soothed them both.

"Are you sure you'll be able to kill it?" she asked.

Kenji sighed. "A year ago, I would have said no. Now. I'm not sure. There's a chance. It's been wounded a lot. Maybe, in its weakened state, it will be easier to take down."

"Well, I'm rooting for you all."

"Thanks."

She looked down at herself. "I suppose this will chase away some of those demons you're harboring."

"Time. It's my only remedy."

"Support helps too." She looked at him.

He turned to her. "Are you suggesting I seek counseling?"

She scoffed. "Are you really that blind! Here I have been supporting you all along and you want to seek professional counseling?"

"You're in forensics. Not therapy," he chuckled.

"I don't need to be a therapist to be there for you!"

He looked back at the sea. "No offense, Shu. But I'm just not ready to commit to anything."

Finding herself lost in her thoughts, she shook her head. "How could I have been so selfish."

"It's only natural." Kenji dropped his cigarette on the ground, crushed it, and walked away.

***

Yow entered the hospital room with a look of dismay. He had not had a chance to see his wife since they carted her away in an ambulance. She was still severely singed, and her right eye was swollen. Not to mention the marks, scars, all over her side.

He approached the bed. "Oh, baby."

She turned to him, her head moving slowly. "I'm sorry you have to see me like this."

He did not want to respond in fear of making her misery even more profound. She looked at him with a sadness he had never seen on her before.

"I can't believe this has happened." Her eyes watered.

"You have my word. It won't happen to you or anyone else ever again."

"How can you promise such a thing?"

"We have a couple of plans on how to kill this damn thing. I would be honestly surprised if either one did not work."

"I forbid you to go out on a journey to kill this thing. What about Dede? She needs someone to look after her."

"The hospital's daycare has handled that, and they assure me they'll watch over her while we go out and stop this mockery of nature."

She looked at him with a blank expression. "Is it safe?"

"I'm not going to sugarcoat it. There are risks."

"Who else is going?"

"Morgan. I can't talk him out of it. The sheriff and Kenji are also coming along."

"Let this be the last time," she demanded in a tone that shocked Yow. She was not asking.

"If this plan does not work, I will wash my hands clean of anything to do with the crocodile."

"You promise?"

"I promise." He made his way over to her and gently kissed her blackened forehead.

"Ow."

"Does it hurt?"

"A little."

"We're going to have skin grafts made. Hopefully we can figure something out."

"Just kill the monster."

He nodded and smiled. "Get some sleep. I'll bring Dede by later."

"No. I don't want her to see me like this."

"She will at some point."

"She's probably made friends at the daycare. She's always been able to fit in so nicely with others. Don't rob her of her happiness."

"Ok. We'll play it by ear."

"Thank you." She closed her eyes. Before Yow left, she drifted off to sleep.

***

He had planned the speech for two days. Haruto was now standing amongst what remained of his officers and their dour expressions. They reflected how they felt, like they were fighting a losing war. None of them had signed up to do battle with the scaly menace. For that reason, he requested they all stay on the sidelines for this one.

Here they stood.

"You must all be wondering why me." He paused for dramatic effect. "When I joined the force eleven years ago, I never in my life thought I would be combating a force such as this. There has never been a threat as great in Kowloon before. There is defeat in its future, however. We have a plan. It requires minimal members. I have volunteered myself to join this assault on the crocodile."

"If you can volunteer, why can't we?" one of the officers asked.

"Yeah, you let others join the fray. Hell, Ro even headed the operation," another added.

"Well, now you've seen what happened and heard how quick things could have gone wrong. There were no warnings. No signs of it initiating an attack. It just did. Many have died. I will not lose one more officer or civilian to this thing if I can help it."

The room was silent.

"I think it's time we face facts," Haruto began. "This does not require a lot of people to be on the boat. Too many and I'm afraid we'd slow the ship or, at the very least, have too many shoulders to brush against."

"Then why not just send one of us out?" An officer jumped from his seat. "I volunteer."

"I will *not* have any more deputies killed because of this thing!" Haruto snapped at him. "I can't lose any more of you. We've become a tightknit group. I'd hate for it to shrink further." Haruto let it hang in the air. His decision was final. Everyone began to see that. He then walked away from the podium. Everyone straightened and saluted him. He returned the gesture to each and every one of them.

CHAPTER THREE

An early dawn.

Under the cover of the night, where the only light in Victoria Harbor came from a tall fishing boat, it was steered through the canal and out into the bay area. Every occupant aboard her was afraid yet determined at what lay ahead. Was it certain death? A mighty being ready to cripple them like it had so many others. Crush then until their bodies were no longer recognizable.

Shooting out of the horizon was a light. Several that spread across the sky and dazzled the naked eye. The rays seemed to dance like when one waved a hand in front of a flashlight. The sky itself was not red, which was a good sign. It showed that good weather was most likely to occur over the course of the day.

It was a sharp contrast to how they felt. That urge to turn back was all too great. The crew was ready for anything it seemed. Everything was implemented, the steel hull was durable, the weapons were aboard and ready for action. It was likely they would be successful yet there was doubt amongst them all.

Doubt about the destruction of the crocodile, doubt about their own safety. They even doubted their return to shore.

Kenji had named the boat the Battle Dragon but even he was not convinced of the legitimacy of the plan. He was the captain and made all the choices but, he realized, he had never been in this situation before. Commanding these three men was not the same as having a co-paddler on a canoe. This was a war against a perfect predator. There was no other way around it. The thing had been alive during the time of the dinosaurs, or at least its ancestors. Who's to say it was not indestructible.

A whisp of wind blew past his face as he steered the wheel hard to starboard. The water had a chop to it that he did not like. Heavy waves splashed against the hull and sprayed the air with the salty liquid. Some of it got on Haruto's arm as he sat on the transom. He quickly wiped it off yet continued to stroke his arm. Out of all the men, he was clearly the most nervous.

Morgan looked at him with pity. The lawman was deftly terrified. He was not sure if he had sea legs or if he even knew how to drive a boat. Regardless, they were in this together. He then turned to Yow who was watching the water. He seemed calm and relaxed. Morgan wondered how any man in his predicament could be as such.

"I think you should be more alert," Morgan chuckled nervously.

"I am," Yow argued.

"Okay. Then how can you seem so, I don't know, unaffected by what's happened?"

"You think I don't have Sang in mind?"

"I didn't say that!" Morgan exclaimed.

"There's a time and place for mourning. If you must know, I'm praying."

"With your eyes open?"

"One does not need to be blind in order to understand," Yow argued.

Morgan was silent but not for long. "Do you think this is a suicide mission?"

"That doesn't matter."

"Really? Then what does?" Morgan shouted.

"If we are successful in destroying the crocodile, then it will have been an honor have I to give my life."

Morgan shook his head. "What about your family?"

"They will be safe."

Haruto was having a hard time already with the waves banging against the hull, he did not need the bickering between the two men. He got up and silently walked over to the ladder. Ascending it at a relaxed pace, he figured the view would at least make him less unsettled.

When his feet touched the upper deck, he found himself to be a bit more content.

"Any sign of it?" Kenji asked.

"None." Haruto looked out over the horizon. "Maybe it's gone out to sea, never to return."

Kenji shook his head. "He's not like me. He'll be back."

"What do you mean, not like you?" Haruto asked.

He watched as Kenji steered the wheel a bit to the port side, adjusting the vessel. The man was stoic but there was something eating away at him, chipping his armor like a musket ball striking the steel plate.

"I had a second chance," Kenji said suddenly.

"A second chance for what?"

"I was not the only survivor on Habito Island."

"That's what your report said."

"Yes, well. I managed to rescue an infant. After I left the island, I brought him to an orphanage and dropped him off. He did not need to know the horrors that happened there."

"That's admirable." Haruto nodded.

"Yes. I still can't help but feel I gave him up when I shouldn't have. He needed a family, and I needed someone to relate to."

"You can't dump what happened on him."

"No. I think he at least deserves to know what happened."

"Maybe." Haruto looked out over the water again. "When you get back you'll have a choice to make."

"I have a couple to make."

"Now what's the problem?" Haruto laughed.

"Shu."

"Shu?"

"I gave her the cold shoulder."

"Well, you'll need to fix that. Or, at the very least, clear the air."

"I tried but wasn't very nice about it." Kenji lowered his head.

"Mistakes happen. You have to fix the problems you cause before it's too late."

This time, Kenji nodded.

Victoria Bay disappeared in the haze as Kowloon became a line of land. The distance was ever growing, the expansive expedition into elimination.

It was purely out of the blue when they heard a boat motor speeding towards them. Kenji had heard it first and turned to see a small dinghy practically hovering over the water as it crossed the wide-open area.

"Who's that?" Haruto noticed the boat next.

"Don't know," Kenji stated.

"Maybe it's another fisherman?" Morgan called up to them.

"Then why is he speeding our way?" Kenji shot a glance down at Morgan before returning his attention to the small watercraft.

"Whoever he is, he shouldn't be out here," Haruto stated.

Kenji brought the Battle Dragon to a slow. Water lapped against her hull in a rhythmic motion. Soon, she was at a full stop. It gave the speedboat enough time to make it towards them.

There was a driver, a local. The passenger was wearing a straw hat and had his head tilted down towards them. When they were close enough to toss a line, the man looked up.

"Mako?" Haruto shouted.

"Surprise," the reporter smiled cheekily.

"You cannot be here!"

"C'mon, Sheriff. I have a story to finish. Besides, you don't want your mission to go undocumented. This is a monstrous occasion, pardon the pun."

"You sound like you prepared that statement," Yow mumbled.

"The whole trip out," Mako laughed.

Both boats sat idling next to one another, yet no one aboard either made a move.

Kenji turned to Haruto. "We don't need more men."

Sensing the displeasure at his presence, Mako decided to sweeten the deal. "I have a chopper on standby in case we need to be evacuated."

"Your editor really pulled out all the stops, huh?" Morgan said.

"We need this story."

"We or you?" Yow asked.

"Everyone," Mako clarified.

"Well then, I suggest you get that chopper of yours and scout the area. We don't need more men," Haruto told him.

"C'mon, Sheriff. I also have my sea legs and won't get in the way." He winked at them.

"Do you know how to use guns?"

"Probably better than half of you aboard this ship," Mako chuckled.

Haruto shared a glance with Kenji. "It's your call, Captain."

Kenji scoffed at the reporter. "Get your gear and climb aboard. I don't have all day."

With spry steps, Mako practically leapt aboard the Battle Dragon. He waved off the boatman who began to back away.

"Will he be alright?" Yow asked.

"Who, him?" Mako gestured to the boatman. "He probably knows the waters better than even Kenji over here."

"Fat chance," Kenji snarled and started the ignition again.

The boatman waved them off and sped back towards the shore. Kenji figured he had a good hour and a half to reach the mainland. He gave him a silent prayer and turned back to the horizon. The blue skies were spread further out, and the sun was beaming down on them. The serene, picturesque majesty of it all brought him comfort. He hoped it would last for the rest of the morning.

***

Pressing forward, not daring to look back, the boatman was pleased with himself. He had made a nice bundle of Yuan and would be able to keep the lights on at his shack and gas in his tank for at least another two months. Not to mention that he would be able to catch fish to fill his belly with or sell on the market. He hoped for the latter. He grew tired of the gifts from the sea and would love a nice pork dinner. Spare ribs were calling his name.

The pleasant thought of a well-cooked meal was suddenly forgotten when he saw a water spray off in the distance. It was a rather large gush of water. Too big to be a whale. It shot up almost thirty feet, frothing and dissipating in the air. He stared at the general area where it occurred with defiance. There was a good chance it was the crocodile. It was all too likely that it was there to rob him of his riches in life and wealth. He was not a particularly lucky person.

Another spout of water came about fifty feet to his left. Either it was two of the biggest whales known to man, or the crocodile was incredibly fast. The water rocketing out of its nose was almost an instigation tactic he felt. It was urging him to try and escape when he knew himself there was none.

"Damn you," he said, coldly.

He sat there and watched for what felt like an eternity. The dread of not knowing where it would come from next ate away at the boatman. When it did finally happen again, it was right below him.

The motorboat flew into the air from the water pressure pressing against the wooden hull. He gripped both sides tightly so that he would not shake from side to side. He happened to peer down, expecting to see the frothing sea. Instead, what he saw was its cavernous mouth.

Before he could scream, the boat landed in the parted jaws that quickly snapped shut over the boat. They crushed the bow and stern, splintering the wood as the watercraft was made out of toothpicks. The midportion of it began to slide down its gullet. The boatman scrambled to find a way to escape. He felt around, touching the slimy roof of the crocodile's mouth. He looked but found that, even if he found a solid surface, the interlocked teeth kept him inside like a prison.

He screamed before disappearing into an opening. Soon he found the stomach where he would be trapped until decomposed and digested.

It caught their attention right away. The very sight of the water spray was enough for everyone aboard the Battle Dragon to turn their head in unison in its general direction. It was hard to miss. Several more followed and then it happened. The boatman was consumed by the fierce fiend.

While everyone else gasped in shock and awe, Kenji's reaction was minute by comparison. He had seen this happen far too often. Still, it was such a sight that it caused him to react, just not in the same way as everyone else. As they all stared in bewilderment, he reached for the wheel and turned hard to starboard.

Haruto had witnessed the crocodile in the swamp. While the area was claustrophobic and the surrounding mangroves and brush was a tight fit, it was still condensed. The crocodile looked mighty up close. From far away, it was a gargantuan. Yow too had seen the crocodile up close and personal. Nothing could prepare him for just how big the animal was.

Morgan began to stumble back. This creature was not meant to be. No crocodile was this big in modern times. Perhaps it was larger than its massive ancestors. When the boat began to turn, so did the crocodile. It faced them head on. He attempted to gage just how large the animal was. It was a rough estimate, but he figured the crocodile to be thirty meters. Nearly one hundred feet!

"We're not equipped to handle this," he said solemnly.

Mako was busy snapping photographs to really take in the threat of what was happening. The boat and crocodile were closing the gap between them. It was only a matter of minutes before they would collide.

"Kenji, stop the boat," Haruto ordered.

The captain did not acknowledge him.

"You wanted a battle," Yow stated matter-of-factly.

"This is insane!" Morgan yelled.

"You're not giving up on me, on my mother! Are you?" Yow turned in his direction.

"No. But we need a better strategy then just ramming it full force!" Morgan shouted.

"Any suggestions?" Kenji called down to him.

The clicking of Mako's camera was the only thing that made a noise.

"What if we lure it instead of chase it," Haruto continued. "We could bring it over towards the Mai Po River and corner it in its own home."

"That worked so well last time," Kenji practically laughed in his face.

"We didn't have explosives last time," Haruto brought up.

"There's no way this thing will fall for the same trick twice," Morgan shouted. "Crocodiles are smart. They know where they can feed and where to keep away from."

"You know what. Fuck this!" Kenji screamed. "Get the mesh netting ready. We're going to toss it on the damn thing on a pass by."

Everyone but Mako snapped into action. He was now on the pulpit staring at the oncoming force as if it were a freight train. There was no sign of fear in him. Haruto found it admirable as he put on his gloves. He, along with Morgan, then lowered the razor wire into the water and fed it out further.

Yow exited the cabin with a dart gun.

"Should we use the bait?" Morgan asked.

"There's no time," Yow yelled as he loaded a dart into the chamber.

Time seemed to slow suddenly. Yow made his way over to the port-side bow and steadied himself.

The gap was merely fifty feet by the time he took his first shot. It struck the crocodile on the back and bounced off its scaly hide.

"You need to aim lower. Under the belly or in the mouth!" Morgan called to him as he watched over his shoulder.

"Just wait until we get the thing in the net before you start firing!" Haruto suggested angrily.

Without any sign of it performing the maneuver, the crocodile slipped under the surface.

"Did it just sink?" Mako shouted, disappointedly.

"They can do that. They can be near you without even making a ripple on the surface," Morgan explained.

"Stay alert, everyone!" Haruto called out.

True to his word, there was no ripple when the crocodile rammed into the steel hull of the fishing boat. Kenji struggled to steer her in the opposite direction in order to keep it from capsizing. Mako was quick on his feet and scurried down the pulpit. He managed to get over to the harpoon gun and searched his person for a lighter.

"Don't touch that!" Kenji noticed him.

"I've got this!" Mako yelled.

After an attempt that took longer than it should have, Mako produced the lighter. He then ignited the fuse attached to the stick of dynamite on the harpoon. Then, pointing it at the water, he stood and waited. As he pushed himself off of the weapon to steady himself, he got a better view of the immediate area.

"Well! Turn the damn thing!" Kenji cried out.

"I don't know if it'll get caught in the net!" Mako explained.

A huge wave crashed against the hull sending a salty shower over the men.

"It wants a challenge, does it!" Kenji laughed in defiance.

"That was just the sea!" Morgan explained.

"No, my friend. It's trying to use natural phenomena to wash us off the boat!" Kenji slowed the vessel.

"You're mad!" Morgan stated. "Speed back up! It won't get cut up as much if the net just taps it."

A few yards off the bow, the crocodile breached the surface. Its jaws snapped wildly. It was clear it was coming straight up for them.

Mako did not waste his golden opportunity. He shot the harpoon, sending the projectile flying through the air and into the crocodile's front left armpit. The explosion sent the boat and the crocodile in opposite directions. He quickly sat up. "Take that, you green bastard!"

Red water appeared from below. It was steadily rising in a gushing fashion. Then, something else surfaced. It was a scaly clawed appendage.

"Is that its foot?" Yow asked.

"… And a little of its arm too!" Morgan laughed in surprise.

"What do ya know!" Haruto turned to Kenji and grinned. "You can kill a god."

CHAPTER FOUR

A demon from the past.

It was a long time waiting before Kenji determined it was official. The crocodile was not resurfacing with a furious comeback. It did not return the damage caused to it by attacking the boat, smashing it to pieces, and devouring the occupants. Instead, the choppy waves soon gave way to the calm sea.

There was no doubt in his mind. It was finally over. Morgan felt his legs begin to buckle. A weight was lifted off his chest as he exhaled loudly. His exasperated breath was followed by a victorious yell. Yow followed suit while Haruto hollered with delight. Mako had not seen such enthusiasm in a long time. All four men were cheering. All the while, his story was going to be a short but memorable one. He could see the headlines now. *Local reporter defeats giant crocodilian menace.* He smiled at the thought.

It was late afternoon by the time they were sure of its defeat. Yow had fished out the foot, letting Morgan examine it in the cabin below. His friend sat by him with keen interest.

"Yep. Judging by my calculations, the animal is thirty meters long."

Yow whistled. "A monster."

"A god," Kenji said as he appeared in the doorway.

"God's can't die, Mr. Ho," Morgan corrected him.

"Then maybe it's a demon, cast out of hell," Kenji stated.

"Have a look." Morgan held up the severed foot. "It's not alive. If the foot and arm are missing, there's likely a crater on its side. It's bled out by now and sank to the bottom."

"When will we know for sure?" Kenji asked.

"It takes a while for the body to fill up with gas," Yow explained.

"Good thing we have a doctor aboard." Kenji gave a half smirk.

Yow did not like the man's tone but brushed it off.

"I think we should stay until the body bloats and surfaces," Morgan suggested. "It is a monster, but it is also a scientific anomaly that cries out for study."

"Can it be done?" Yow asked. "Can we actually drag it to shore?"

"I'm sure my winch will hold. Especially if the creature's missing a chunk out of it." Kenji patted under his armpit. "Probably a great deal lighter."

The three men nodded.

Mako sat on the pulpit as he took pictures of the setting sun. The dazzling display of reds and oranges brought about a peaceful serenity. Mako did not break away from his camera though. He always figured that he could enjoy the moment through a lens and be able to hold onto it forever printed on a photograph.

The only caveat to his relaxation. He had been thinking about it for the past few hours now. A guilt that ate at him like cancer. He kept returning to his camera, but never once did it feel right.

"Getting any good ones?" Haruto called out to him.

The reporter nearly jumped out of his skin. He spun to see the sheriff standing at the beginning of the pulpit with a concerned look on his face.

"I'm sorry. I did not mean to startle you," he apologized.

"It's no problem." Mako stood up and began to make his way onto the deck of the bow. "Yes. I'm sure they'll come out dazzling."

"They better. You've been out there for an hour now," Haruto chuckled.

Mako gave a nod and then made his way past the lawman.

"I get it," Haruto said suddenly.

"Get what?"

"The guilt," he continued. "You hired a boatman to bring you out here. Now he's dead and you know now that you're responsible."

"He came at his own free will."

"Really? How much did you pay him?"

"That's besides the point," Mako said.

"Is it? I doubt he would have done it so freely if he was not paid."

Mako thought about it for a moment. "I suppose you're right."

"I know it's hard. I've unknowingly sent officers, good men, to their deaths a handful of times. It never gets any easier."

"How do you cope with it?"

Haruto sighed. "I tell myself that they signed up for the job. It makes it only slightly less painful."

"How do I live with myself after what I did?"

"You couldn't have known the crocodile would kill him."

"Yeah, but I should have." Mako lowered his head.

Haruto placed a hand on the man's shoulder. "You killed the crocodile. As far as I am concerned, you avenged his death."

Mako smiled. "I guess so."

"I know so. Now get some rest. We're staying out here until the damn thing comes to the surface, dead as a doornail," Haruto told him.

The reporter saluted the sheriff as he walked away. He then turned and took one more picture of the sunset before retreating into the cabin.

***

Plop.

The sound was so soft that no one heard it. Even after several others occurred. Everyone was fast asleep. The threat was gone, there was no need for a guard.

Each man had different dreams yet they were all similar in a way. They all involved the crocodile and the death and destruction it caused. Their eyes shifted in their nightmares as they looked about for ways of rescue and escape.

Kenji panted as he raced to find a way out of the predicament that haunted him. Deep down, he accepted his family was dead and village destroyed. Now there was only one thing to do. Survive.

Yow and Morgan both dreamt of similar scenarios. They had not yet accepted that Lilly was dead and Sang injured. Instead, their dreams were focused on saving their loved ones.

Haruto dreamt of going home to find his wife and daughter gone. They moved on after he had died. In his disillusioned state, he had been ravaged by the crocodile like Pat's floppy corpse being shook around. Yet he lived. No one knew. Part of him felt he was still dead. Perhaps an apparition, doomed to haunt his family till the day they died.

Mako saw his whole world figurately turned upside down. His life, job, and income had all been swept away in one massive blow by the crocodile. His place of work was swept away by a tidal wave where the reptile seemed to lead the charge of water. It seemed so outlandish, yet it was happening.

Plop. Plop. Plop.

The sound began to intensify. It was a wall of noise that carried with it a thunderous explosion. Everyone shot up in the cabin, startled by the noise.

"Is that rain?" Mako asked.

"What happened to the clear skies?" Morgan wondered.

"Oh no," Kenji said.

All eyes looked to him.

The droplets of water pelted the boat as Kenji stood up from his cot. The sound was deafening. He waited for a flash of the lightning to occur. There was nothing but the blackness of night as far as he could see. He feared the worst. The crocodile could indeed conjure up bad weather, affecting and bending it to its own will and desire.

Howling wind then began to whisp past the Battle Dragon. Gadgets and other materials began to whip around. Even the harpoon gun rattled in its foundation a bit. The bell to alert other fishing vessels of nearness was also dinging incessantly.

A sudden bright white light flashed before Kenji's eyes. It was somewhat faint but enough for him to see. The mainland was not visible. They were too far out. It was there though. Hiding amongst the surf. Its eyes glowed red with an intense fury. He noticed it was a bit lopsided, likely due to the missing foot.

"My god," Kenji said coldly.

"What is it?" Morgan asked, worriedly.

Kenji turned slowly to his crew. "We're not done yet."

Thunderous rage boomed outside. It caused them to quickly get off their cots and snap into action. Under one of the blankets, Mako pulled out his camera. The others found weapons stashed in various places. Mostly firearms but they were all they had.

They then turned to Kenji whose solemn expression told them everything. "I think we should pray."

"There's no time!" Haruto stated as he made his way out of the cabin.

Yow followed close behind. While Morgan seemed apprehensive, Mako was busy putting his camera together.

"What do we do? Shoot it?" Morgan asked.

"We have to do something," Kenji ordered as he grabbed the man by the arm and guided him out of the cabin.

The weather above was most unwelcoming. The powerful gusts caused everything to flap around, including Kenji's long black hair. He continuously had to brush it out of his face. On one of the wipe aways, he caught a glimpse of the crocodile. One that was too late.

It rammed into the side of the boat full force. It began to tilt to the starboard side, reaching closer and closer to the waterline.

"Kenji! Get on the wheel!" Haruto ordered him as he took the first shot at the animal.

Yow followed suit. The crocodile seemed to retreat from the gunfire. Both men's cheers turned to screams as its massive tail came down and slammed along the portside, taking out the guardrail.

"Fuck!" Haruto shouted in amazement.

Mako exited the cabin then. He was not carrying his camera but, rather, he wore a look of excitement. He made his way over towards the bow and situated himself near the harpoon.

"What are you doing?" Kenji asked.

"I'm going to make the front page!" Mako laughed.

The boat was rocking back and forth now on account of the crocodile and the weather it brought with it. Mako was having a hard time not slipping. The last thing he wanted was to fall into the water moments before his big moment.

It was clear the crocodile was there, staring at Mako. The man was the most active on deck. While everyone was firing the weapons at it, this man was doing something else. It interested the crocodile enough to go investigate.

Mako reached the weapon and bent over to grab a harpoon in the box they were in. He then quickly loaded it in and aimed. The crocodile was closing in, fast.

"You got this, Mako!"

"You're damn right!" he cheered.

The vessel was bobbing up and down and side to side. The shot was going to be tricky. He not only had to account for the trajectory but the movement of the ship. He felt around his person for his lighter.

"Hurry up!" Haruto ordered.

He checked his pant pockets before reaching into his shirt one. Locating it at the very bottom, he quickly pulled it out and leaned forward. Flicking at the striker, he waited for the flame to appear. The rain was making it difficult for it to stay lit long enough to light the fuse attached to the dynamite on the spear. The crocodile was now several yards away.

"Damnit, man! Shoot the thing!" Yow called to him.

Kenji watched in abstract horror as a flash of lightning revealed the crocodile was not there anymore. "Where'd it go?"

Morgan came out of the cabin. "I'll get the spotlight on it."

Climbing up the ladder, he stood at the consol. Soon, a strong beam of light shot out of the device, and he pointed it where Mako stood.

"Turn it towards the water!" Mako ordered.

He did so. The waves were choppy but there was nothing in them that was visible to the naked eye.

"It was right there! I could see its eyes!" Mako snarled.

The water soon began to swish swash in an unnatural way. The displacement was all wrong.

"It's coming up!" Kenji shouted.

Mako pointed it down. He should have pointed up. The crocodile exploded from the water. It was not content with being bound to the sea for in that moment, it was airborne. It soared high over the vessel, propelling itself forward, breaking the laws of science given its sheer weight and size.

Morgan saw the crocodile charging for him, jaws agape. He quickly ducked down as its jaws slammed shut around the spotlight. Its scaly hide scraped alongside the boat, ripping chunks of wood from it. Its hind foot then got caught on the steering wheel where it ripped it out with one curl of its toes.

"No!" Yow shouted as he watched his friend nearly get taken out by the animal.

The crocodile's tail slammed down next to Mako who fell backwards and rolled onto the deck. It then snapped at the crow's nest, tearing it away from the boat and carrying it into the water along with the spotlight.

An enormous splash concluded the nightmare as it reentered the sea.

CHAPTER FIVE

Dawn brought about clarity.

The early hours of the summer morning gave way to sunlight. It was clear that the ship was in bad shape. The Battle Dragon had suffered specific damage that caused it to drift aimlessly through the sea. Without a wheel, there was no guidance. Without the crow's nest, there was no good view of the mainland.

Mako stood by the harpoon gun which was now in shambles. The crocodile's tail had practically torn the bolts out and took it back into the sea with it. It had been pulled across the deck but got caught on one of the guardrails. The reporter looked defeated, as if he were a kid whose toy had been stolen by some bully. He had gone back into the cabin and found his camera he had placed in one of the portholes on the ground, smashed beyond repair. The film was no good. He had it set on a timer. Even if the shot was taken, it was no good now.

Kenji assessed the situation further. There was debris from the guardrail on the starboard side littering the deck. The boat had taken a beating. Yet she was still afloat. Ready for battle as far as he was concerned.

"What are we going to do now?" Morgan shouted.

"We're going to finish the job," Kenji ordered.

"With what?" Morgan whined.

"We still have dynamite, some machine guns. We can do this," he replied stubbornly.

Ripe with a newfound sense of defeat, Morgan made his way towards the stern and sat on the transom. "I don't think we can."

"I beg your pardon?" Yow turned to his friend. "We owe my mom at least another attempt."

Morgan looked down at himself. "I can still sense her presence. I want to keep her memory alive."

"We have photographs for that. For now, we need to kill this crocodile!" Yow argued.

Haruto walked out of the cabin below. He had been using the bilge pump to get some of the water out from below and his shoes were now soaked. "If we can't stop it, who can?"

"We should've called in the military a long time ago," Morgan said.

"All these attempts were not in vain. It's injured!" Haruto snapped at the man.

"Even so. It would have all been over sooner if we got a submersible down there." He pointed a finger over his shoulder at the water.

"I don't want mutiny aboard my boat," Kenji said. "We need to work together. We're going to try the poisoned bait idea."

"Humph," Morgan scoffed.

An hour later the bait was set. There was poison and dynamite attached to a large chunk of pig carcass. If one did not work, the other surely would. Yow had gathered enough strychnine from the hospital to kill a herd of elephants.

Mako shouldered a rifle. His one job now was to hit the dynamite. There was no way to light the fuse once it was out there.

"If you can't hit the explosives, my strychnine will do the trick." Yow smiled and patted him on the back.

He then walked over towards Kenji "Are we near any coral reefs?"

"No. The charts show there's a bed about a mile out but we're far enough away so that the poison won't cause any damage."

"Excellent!" Yow clapped his hands together. "Alright, Morgan. Lower the bait."

His friend gave him a look but still followed his order. The bait hit the water, and pinkish viscera began to spread out. The plasma reached a decent distance before it was lifted and dropped again in a bobbing motion.

"Come get breakfast!" Morgan said, staring at the water, his eyes frenziedly searching the waves for the first sign of disturbance.

The wait was not long.

It tugged on the bait and pulled it down. The line spooled out of the winch in rapid succession. Morgan cheered as did everyone else, but Mako who kept his sights on where the bait once was.

Snap.

A sharp cracking sound was heard as the length of wire ran out and tugged on the winch. The Battle Dragon then began to move seemingly on her own.

"Looks like this bitch is taking us for a ride!" Morgan yelled.

"Good! Let it tire itself out!" Yow shouted back.

"That shouldn't be too long," Morgan continued. "Crocodiles are slower on land than in the water. If it keeps going this speed, it'll use up its energy faster than if we were fishing for it in the Mai Po River on some sandbank."

Kenji and Haruto both ignored the jab. It was not insulting. This idea seemed to be working better anyway.

A waterspout suddenly shot up as the crocodile expelled water from its nose.

"There it blows!" Morgan cried out in excitement.

Mako looked down the barrel of the rifle. The crocodile was not facing them. He could not take the shot. "The carcass must be fully engulfed. I can't take the shot!"

"We'll wait it out then. If you happen to get the shot, don't hesitate to take it!" Yow ordered.

The crocodile breached the water like a humpback whale, though maneuvering its body in a swaying motion. Its massive girth should have held it back but it seemed to have an advantage over most crocodilians. It was unlike any specimen of its kind. It plowed through the waves with tremendous force, kicking up gouts of water spray. Its massive tail seemed to propel it faster than any creature of its size should allow. It was a true anomaly.

"Thing's surfacing and jumping around as if it were light as a feather," Morgan breathed heavily.

"Not for long," Yow stated.

"It's an incredible sight," Mako shouted. "I wish I could get to my spare camera."

Haruto felt like he was not doing anything at the moment and so he disappeared into the cabin below to fetch it.

Kenji watched the skies with stern eyes. Nothing out of the ordinary accumulated in the clouds. Perhaps it could only conjure bad weather in short bursts. It was a thought he prayed was accurate. He turned to see Haruto leaving the cabin with the camera bag.

"Mako! Take some shots. It's not turning anytime soon." He shoved the device into the man's chest.

The reporter lowered the gun and traded it for the camera. Haruto held the gun with no animosity. He knew Mako was a better shot but he realized, if it came to it, he could kill the crocodile just as effectively. He had outclassed most of his officers during target practice in the basement of the station. Only Deputy Ro and a handful of others had better results. All but Ro were dead now.

Furiously snapping away at the crocodile, he managed to capture some breathtaking photos. At least, he hoped so. He would have to wait until they were developed to be sure.

Just then, the line went taut.

"Son of a bitch!" Morgan yelled. "I think the line broke."

Kenji ran over to a compartment near the stern and withdrew a backup miniature motor. He plopped it into the water and steered the Battle Dragon in the right direction. The vessel took longer to reach the destination but at least the target was stationary.

"I think you killed it! It's over!" Haruto cheered.

"I've heard that before," Morgan sighed.

Something became apparent quickly. The body of the crocodile was not greenish black indicating its backside, nor yellow was the underbelly. Instead, the upturned animal had a white back with lines that stretched down the length of its stomach.

"No," Kenji spoke with a coldness so bitter the word felt like ice.

There, in the mouth of a humpback whale, was the pig carcass.

"This doesn't make any sense!" Morgan shouted. "Humpbacks eat plankton."

"Looks like this one got curious." Mako stood up from the deck where he was positioned to get better pictures. "I guess not all whales can be vegan."

"No. Morgan's right. This seems very wrong," Kenji said.

The whale began to move slightly.

"Damn thing's still alive," Haruto stammered.

"Put it out of its misery," Yow said.

Haruto gulped, realizing he wished he had the camera in his possession now instead of the rifle. "Not a lick of good it'll do."

There was never a chance to try. The whale rocketed out of the water as if shot by a high-powered hose. It then descended back down, belly flopping onto the deck of the Battle Dragon. It cracked the steel frame instantly, causing the ship to buckle under its weight. The whale gave out one low, gurgle moan before slipping into the sweet relief of death.

CHAPTER SIX

It was not normal.

The crew of the Battle Dragon were now scrambling around her deck. Trying to figure out how to not end up in the water was pointless while surviving was another level of fear and insanity. The boat was sinking quickly. Whatever damage the crocodile had caused, the humpback had unintentionally finished it.

Morgan looked around dumbfounded. This was no normal reptile. It did not act accordingly nor abide by the laws of nature. Crocodiles were wise, intelligent creatures but this one was different. It used its smarts to strategize on a whole new level. Somewhere between primate and human was this crocodile.

When the inevitable sank in that they were going to sink, Mako ran towards the cabin. He managed to slip in through the splintered wood from the deck. There was still hope, a lifeline. He needed to reach it before the crocodile reached them. He rummaged around and found the radio.

Wham!

An immense force crashed into the boat with the speed and girth of a train. The cabin broke apart and a flow of water came rushing in. Mako spoke like an auctioneer on the radio, desperate to reach his buddies over at the airbase. By the time he heard the first crackle, he saw it. The crocodile was staring at him. It pressed its mighty jaws further into the structure.

"No! Get away from me!"

The predator did not. Instead, it managed to part its mouth slightly as it edged nearer. It was wide enough for Mako to fit in. The reporter cowered in the corner in fear, his bladder releasing then. The lights went out. He was now in the dark, and more afraid than he had ever been. Before he could say his prayers, a bullet came flying in. The flash lit the cabin. The explosive sounds shook the walls. It whizzed by his face and directly at the crocodile who gave a guttural roar of defiance as its orifice yawned wide, breaking through the already smashed ceiling. It was as if it were mocking the bullet wounds, daring them to enter its mouth.

Haruto stood there, shocked. He took another shot, popping several rounds off and into its exposed gums. They seemed to bounce off like Tic Tacs hitting a cement wall. At that moment, he felt hopeless.

Mako edged along the wall before he found himself standing next to Haruto. "We need to go!"

"Go where?" Haruto panicked.

"Anywhere but here!" The reporter grabbed the lawman by the arm and led him out of the cabin.

The lights flickered below as the crocodile shimmied its way out. It then maneuvered itself alongside the boat and was soon swimming again. This time, there was no waiting to study the humans' actions. It was circling them with intent on finishing them off.

It then felt four little bumps on its side. It widened its trajectory and arched its body to its right side where it was tapped. There was nothing there. Then, it happened on its left flank. It squirmed a bit but could not see what was trying to hurt it.

Kenji looked out over the water. "Dolphins!" he cheered.

"What good will they do?" Morgan asked.

"Maybe it's the distraction we need so that the chopper has time to get here," Mako sneered. "If it comes."

"Did you get through to them?" Morgan turned to face the man.

"I don't know."

There was disbelief that covered Morgan's face at that moment. "Then we're screwed!"

"We have time now!" Kenji barked. "Let's make the most of it."

He then disappeared around the gunwale and towards the bow.

"Where's he going?" Morgan was brooding now.

"I don't know," Yow told his friend.

Less than a minute later and Kenji returned with a spear in hand.

"What's that thing going to do against it?" Morgan asked.

The captain ignored him while shoving past. He walked over towards the case of dynamite that was still nestled under the transom and fished out a stick. He then stood up and faced the others. "We have a chance. If we can get it close enough to its brain then, by God, we have a chance."

A faint whirring sound could be heard in the distance. Mako looked out and saw the helicopter closing in. He wanted to smile but his demeanor changed when he looked down. There, wading in the surf, were four mangled dolphin carcasses.

"We have to hurry!" he screamed. "It's going to come back!"

"What about the dolphins?" Morgan asked, his worried tone apparent.

"We'll have to rely on ourselves from here on out."

Haruto discarded the rifle. It was not placed down but rather dropped on the deck. His expression took on one of sheer fright. Yow and Kenji turned but Morgan and Mako did not have a chance to witness the crocodile barreling down on them at full force.

It slammed into the steel hull with little resistance. The plating seemed to aid in the further destruction of the ship. It was knocked in two. The stern split apart from the bow with ease.

An eruption of bullet spray came from the sky; it struck the crocodile with lethal intent. Yet it did little more than annoy it. The pilot angled the helicopter near the splashing bodies in the water as the gunner continued to fire.

"It's gonna get us!" Morgan cried out like a girl.

"Stay calm!" Yow swam over to his friend.

A ladder fell from the helicopter's side door. It landed inches from the water. The pilot brought it down a little lower to allow for easier reach. Morgan was the first to grab it. He stuck one foot in a gap and then used his strength to lift himself forward. His ascent was sluggish.

"Hurry up, man!" Yow called to him.

"Where's the croc?" Haruto called out.

The others looked around and simultaneously felt a sinking feeling in the pits of their stomachs. They knew what it was about to do.

"Pull up!" Yow cried.

Obviously, the pilot could not hear him, but he saw the motions of his hands jabbing upward into the air. He was about to comply when a strong wind current came wisping through.

"You bastard!" Kenji shouted in defiance as he watched the pilot struggle to keep the chopper steady. He could feel the wind rushing past him and could only imagine what it was like for Morgan and, by extension, the pilot.

It came from the right, directly in line with the pilot's view. The crocodile breached the surface. It covered the yard by yard before it was practically standing on its tail. The gunner opened fire on it, aiming for the snout, but it did no good. One last attempt to stop the crocodile that had terrorized Kowloon and the Mai Po River, the pilot dipped the helicopter forward. The rotor blades collided with the crocodile's face, causing a blood mist to shoot up into the clouds. It chopped at the scales, cutting through flesh in some areas. The blades broke apart with each whack. Soon, there was not enough to support the aircraft, and it began to plummet towards the sea.

"Let go!" Yow screamed for his friend who still held onto the ladder.

Morgan was too paralyzed with fear to even comprehend what his friend was saying.

Both crocodile and machine fell back down to their watery graves. The explosion kicked up massive water spray that had splotches of red covering it. The wave towered over the men. There was nowhere to swim away to, nowhere to hide. Kenji tried to move away from the Battle Dragon to avoid being slammed into it. He managed to get five feet before the colossal rush of water came over all of them.

All was black for a time. An aching feeling throbbed in Kenji's head. He tried to open his eyes but the salty sting prevented him from doing so. He realized he was underwater. Forcing his eyes open, they burned, but eventually his vision cleared.

He tried to look up to see the shimmering surface but the entire area around him was red. Blood red. He blew a couple of bubbles and watched them go across his chest. He was upside down. He righted himself and made a mad dash for the surface.

Throat burning, eyes squinting, he grew impatient. He needed air. The sweet relief of oxygen was not there as his lungs burned. He kept bringing his hands over his head, kicking wildly. The challenge proved greater than he ever thought possible.

When the storm had hit Habito, he could have died there. Swept away by the sea, drowning like his family. He hadn't though. He lived while most everyone perished. It must have been Dala's will and desire for him to do so that kept him sane and alive all these years. With this newfound knowledge, he pushed himself to his limit. He could take no more, but he had to. He needed to survive. The reverence of breaching the surface and inhaling a gulp of that sweet, salty air was unmatched.

As soon as he composed himself, he looked around. The Battle Dragon's bow was barely afloat. The lower half was gone, submerged. Probably still sinking towards the bottom. He then saw four forms making their way towards the bow. He smiled with relief.

It quickly disappeared when something surfaced next to him. He nearly leapt out of his skin at the sight of a dead pilot and a mangled gunner. Kenji prayed for their souls, noting their sacrifice. He began to swim over towards the others when he realized he had something in his hand. It was the spear. *No wonder I had a hard time surfacing.* He chuckled at the weapon. The thought of discarding it crossed his mind. Did he really need it? Nothing could survive such a blow. He thought better and kept it.

The five men huddled around the pulpit. It had been snapped in two horizontally. Despite the fractured split, it was still secured to the boat.

"We won?" Morgan spat out saltwater form his mouth.

"Looks like it." Kenji felt relief.

Another body floated to the surface. Its massive girth was stiff as a board. The top of the crocodile's snout had been slashed away leaving nothing but meaty bits and tattered flesh.

"Go to hell," Kenji told the animal.

Then, it squirmed.

"It's still alive!" Morgan's tone was both shocked and in disbelief.

The crocodile turned slowly as it faced the men. It let out a low, gurgled roar. It approached slow at first. The momentum picked up as its tail propelled it forward. It was going to hit the left side where Yow and Morgan were.

Kenji acted quicker than he ever thought he could. He ascended the snapped pulpit and held the spear out, using the rail for leverage. He then looked down at Haruto and Mako.

"Push it in this direction!" he ordered.

The two men kicked frantically. Their tired legs only able to move it so fast, they were not making progress. The crocodile was closing the gap. Morgan swam around to aid the others while Yow kept the crocodile in place. He was the new bait.

Forcing the bow to move towards it, the men watched as the crocodile pivoted to the right.

"Clever croc!" Morgan muttered.

The three men then swam around where Yow was. They treaded water, waiting for the animal to give chase. It kept on its line of sight, aiming off to the right more.

"We're going to miss it!" Yow snarled.

Kenji looked down at the harpoon and then hefted it onto his shoulder. "Eat this!"

He threw it with all his might. It landed on its face, hitting its eye, causing it to rupture. The fleshy remains fell into the water. The crocodile turned and wasted no time in charging again. Its aim was off now.

"Now!" Kenji cried as he hopped up and down to lower the bow to be level with the crocodile.

Jaws yawning wide, the beast slammed into the boat. The pulpit fractured instantly and slid up the roof of its mouth. The splintered wood cracked through flesh, bone, muscle, and then its scaly skin as it rammed through its brain and impaled it out the top of its head.

The men screamed in unison for minutes on end. All out of defiance, hate, and alleviation.

CHAPTER SEVEN

The nightmare was over.

After three grueling hours trapped out at sea, a coastguard cutter arrived to pick them up. They were due to check in that afternoon. When they did not, the mighty vessel was sent out. They were found in a current near a reef.

Yow had made a point to observe the sea life teeming below. The water was much clearer than the bay area and Mai Po River. The dazzling spectacle below instilled a sense of peace and victory. They had destroyed the crocodile without harming the reefs. His one last semblance of hope was kept. He felt content to return home where they would sing their praises.

Morgan was silent after the crocodile was dead. He had not spoken a word while wading in the water nor when they boarded the cutter. To him, there was not much to say. They were successful but it was too little too late. Lilly was dead. When they entered Victoria Harbor, he finally yielded to his pent-up emotions. His tears spilled down his cheeks until they ran dry.

Mako's chief editor stood in the harbor with a look of satisfaction on his face. Yet he himself felt no such glee. He had not only led the boatman to his death, but the pilot and gunman as well. When they docked, he handed him his materials as well as his reporter identification. He did not ask for credit. He did not want the blood-soaked success.

Haruto met up with a couple of his deputies who reported that they sent out a search party the second the time passed, and he had not checked in. He nodded and told them there would be a time to celebrate and thank them all personally. At that moment, they had a carcass to parade around.

Kenji stepped off the cutter with a blanket wrapped around him. He was cold but not on the outside. He could feel his insides were bitter. He had accepted that Dala was with him in spirit, yet he had not fully moved on. That all changed when he saw Shu on the dock. Her smile was as big as her heart. He walked slowly towards her and the two then embraced.

The crocodile was hoisted up onto a partially submerged portion of the dock. Several scientists and reporters crowded around the anomaly of nature. Kenji and Shu passed them. They both knew, deep down, it would burn in hell forevermore.

***

Three weeks later at the Kowloon Orphanage, one of the largest ones in all of Hong Kong, a modestly dressed woman walked down the hallway. She entered a room labeled *Young Youths* and perused through the sleeping infants. She stumbled upon the one she was assigned to retrieve and then made her way out towards the lobby. She eventually found an office where two people, a man and a woman, were sitting across from the orphanage director.

"Here he is," she told them.

Kenji turned to see the bundle of joy wrapped in a white blanket. His heart melted.

It had been achieved thanks to Mako. He asked the paper for one favor before he departed. To print the story of Kenji and the island of Habito. It captured the hearts of the region so much so that greater effort was put into finding the child.

"He looks so much like his parents." Kenji cupped his mouth, forcing himself not to cry.

The nurse carefully handed him the child.

"Thank you," he told her.

"Thank Mako." The director beamed.

"I will." Kenji nodded. He then turned to Shu. "Thank you for coming."

"I couldn't let you do this alone." She smiled.

The two exited the orphanage. Kenji carried the infant with pride. He had given up all hope in his life. In a way, he was happy the crocodile had returned and was now destroyed. It gave him the ability to move on. He would never forget what happened on Habito nor the family and loved ones he lost.

The legend, the curse of the Crocodilian was now being examined by the top minds in the field. No one had a logical explanation as to its size and aggression as of yet. It was an anomaly that Kenji could pry himself from.

Shu placed her head on Kenji's shoulder as he drove them home. Not to Kenji's dank, dismal shack but Shu's place. It was much cleaner there. The appearance was not the only thing he looked forward to. He kissed Shu on the head as he pulled the car into the driveway.

***

The airport was crowded with those who come and those who go. Morgan was the latter. He had stayed in Kowloon long enough. The time he spent was dedicated to Yow and his family. Sang had been released from the hospital and was now at home. It took time for Dede to adjust to the change in her appearance, but it was not long. She tended to her mom as if her parent were the child.

Now, he stood in the waiting area to board the plane.

"Are you sure you can't stay?" Yow asked.

"I've been a burden long enough."

"Nonsense! It's been our pleasure." Yow bowed in thanks.

Morgan did the same.

The intercom dinged, announcing the onboarding. Morgan looked up at the ceiling as if he could see the voice buzzing through the speaker.

"I want to thank you," Yow said.

"For what?" Morgan asked.

"For making my mom happy."

Yow could see a tear fall down his eye.

"She made me happy too." Morgan placed a hand on his friend's shoulder and the two embraced.

When they parted, Yow held out a Polaroid. In the photograph was a picture of Lilly only much younger than Morgan had ever seen her.

"Take this." Yow handed it to Morgan. "For comfort."

"I'll never let it go." He smiled in response and then walked in line with the rest of the passengers.

Yow watched him until he disappeared from view. He then waited until his plane took off, waving his goodbyes.

***

Haruto sat in his office. His whole world had been changed by the events that occurred on that boat. He was never a religious man but, seeing that beast mercilessly attack again and again as if it enjoyed it made him think the crocodile were haunted, possessed by some supernatural force.

If there were such entities, what else was out there?

Mayor Lee had released the ban, and the beaches were open again. Haruto could only hope and pray that there would never be another catastrophe of this scale again. Nearly a hundred casualties, ninety-seven to be exact based on the findings so far. It was almost too many to fathom.

His deputies celebrated his return, the achievement of killing the crocodile, and his success with not dying. They cheered and sang shanties. It was a glorious time. All but for one.

Deputy Ro was nowhere to be found. He had been hospitalized for a few days but then vanished. No trace, no notice. He was just gone. Haruto had worried but figured he could use the sick time.

It was now four weeks later. He had to file him for job abandonment. He had not contacted him so there was no telling if he was alright or not.

Haruto sighed as he opened the morning paper to read through it. In a small column he merely passed over was an article on the rise of satanic hysteria.

***

The red hallway glowed with an ominous mystique. There was something dark about it that exuberated evil. Orange flames flickered on wax sticks on tables going down it. It was not the very sight of gloom and hate that signified the desire but the very intentions of the room at the end of the hall.

It was blackness in a 72X24 frame. There was no source of light coming from it. Any kind of insidious sights came further inside, down a cobblestone walkway with red brick sidings on the surrounding walls. It was through a door, black and unmarked, that real horror lay.

A cloaked figure in a red robe entered the room carrying an object roughly the size of a football. Behind him were two other men and a crazed individual between them. This person was covered in a brown robe, as if they were some sort of monk. There was nothing religious about the once civilized human being. Instead, he thrashed between them in a fit of rage.

The leader of the sullen group began to chant over the cries. Waling so loud, their voices carried down the hall. Eventually, they passed a curtain where several other robed figures stood in a V-shape. At the highest point of the line was a table. The leader approached what appeared to be an altar of sorts and placed the white object down.

Everyone began to chant. *"Rise. Rise, crocodilian. Rise!"*

"He has gifted us with his presence," the robed man in front said as he neared the table. His voice was deep and menacing.

The shrine had chunks of crocodile scale-laden skin situated in a triangular position. As he stood before it, he lifted an oval object overhead.

"Crocodilian rise. Make them fall." He then lowered it down and placed it gently on the table just as the first cracking sounds could be heard.

As he moved out of the way, the two others brought the shaking figure closer. They sat him down, pushed him forward so that he was leaning over the table. They then pulled the burlap sack they had over his head and removed the hood of his robe.

Ro, deputy of the sheriff's department in Kowloon, Hong Kong, had a smile etched on his face that would make babies cry.

"Will you sacrifice your life's juices to bring it into the world?" the deep voiced figure asked him.

"I never had any purpose in life. Not until the other one let me live. I thought I was rising the ranks when I was put in charge of the plan. I ended up failing. Still, it let me live," Ro explained.

"What will you do when it's born?"

Ro began to laugh maniacally. "Worship. Oh yes! Worship the god incarnate!"

He held out his own head over the egg to witness its birth firsthand. Then, a white-hot flashing sensation seared across his throat. He did not break his concentration even as blood spilled from his neck. Copious amounts of plasma fluid began to rush down in little red rivers. Instead of reeling back in abject horror, he lifted his head up even higher to let the blood spray onto the egg.

It rained down as the cracks became more apparent. Every hooded figure suddenly gasped as the snout poked through. It was a sight to behold. The snout was black as night. The crimson substance continued to splash down onto the hatchling as it opened its mouth, accepting its new gift. The gift of life.